L. Travis teaches English at a Minnesota college and lectures frequently on fantasy and literature.

Ben and Zack Series, Book 3

Redheaded Orphan

L. Travis

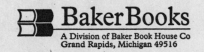

Baker Books
A Division of Baker Book House Co
Grand Rapids, Michigan 49516

Published by Baker Books
a division of Baker Book House Company
P.O. Box 6287, Grand Rapids, Michigan 49516-6287

Printed in the United States of America

Library of Congress Cataloging-in-Publication Data

Travis, Lucille, 1931–
    Redheaded orphan / L. Travis.
      p.   cm. —(Ben and Zack series ; bk. 3)
    Summary: In 1864 when his family moves to Bellfield, Minnesota, where his father will be the town minister, twelve-year-old Ben misses his friend Zack, who is now a drummer in the Union Army, but he finds a new friend in an orphan whose parents were killed during an Indian raid.
    ISBN: 0-8010-4023-X
    [1. Frontier and pioneer life—Minnesota—Fiction. 2. Minnesota—Fiction. 3. Orphans—Fiction. 4. Christian life—Fiction. 5. United States—History—Civil War, 1861–1865—Fiction. 6. Indians of North America—Minnesota—Fiction.] I. Title. II. Series: Travis, L., 1931–   Ben and Zack series ; bk. 3.
    PZ7.T68915Re   1995
    [Fic]—dc20   95-3137

To Phil and Bry and Chris
who gave me all that is the best
of Ben and Jamie

Contents

Prologue

How It All Started

The war party of Sioux Indians attacked shortly after darkness fell. The boy in the outhouse at the edge of the woods heard thc cries of the warriors as they rode toward the cabin. Under cover of the noise he managed with trembling hands to loosen a board in the back wall, crawl through, and hide in the woods. From a thicket he saw his pa come to the cabin door. Gunshots rang out, and in the light that streamed from the cabin he saw his father fall. His mothcr rushed out to help and fell under the heavy firing. In a few moments his grandfather and grandmother, too, lay on the ground beside his parents. Stunned the boy stayed crouched in the woods. When the braves mounted their ponies and rode out they left the cabin burning behind them.

Out of the shadows a silent figure slipped next to the boy, and a strong brown hand covered his mouth. "Make no sound. Little Crow's warriors hear well. We must wait."

Twisting around, the boy, Jamie, saw the face of his Indian friend Joseph. Slowly Joseph took his hand away. "Do not fear. John Other Day comes."

As Joseph spoke the Indian called John Other Day, well known for his friendship to the settlers, joined them. When the sound of the ponies' hoofbeats had faded John Other Day stood. "Stay here with Joseph," he commanded. "I will return." The Indian left as silently as he had come. In a few minutes he was back.

"You must be brave," he said to the boy. "Your father was a good man. Your mother a good woman. Their death was swift."

Jamie wept openly. "Grandpa and Grandma too?" he asked choking on the words.

"They have gone together to our Father's house in the sky," John Other Day answered.

"Why did they do it?" the boy whispered. Tears rolled down his face as the terrible scenes of the night came back. "Ma and Pa, Grandpa—they didn't have a chance." Sobs choked his voice. "What my people do is bad," Joseph said. "They do not know the Great Father or his son. Their bellies are filled with hatred of the white men who cheat them. You must be brave like your father, a good man." Joseph touched the boy's red hair and called him by the name he had given him when his father first brought his small son to visit the Indian camp. "Come, Little Red Fox, we must walk."

Joseph and John Other Day spoke quietly for a moment. "Others will need help," John Other Day said. "You will be safe with Joseph, Little Red Fox."

"Come," Joseph said motioning. "We go to the missionary's house across the river. From there you will go to the fort." As if in a dream Jamie followed. They moved quickly, and suddenly the boy's foot caught in a tree root, which sent him sprawling. Pain shot through his ankle.

"Not good," Joseph said feeling the swelling flesh around the foot. With a swift motion he hoisted the boy to his shoulder. For hours they kept to the woods away from the settlements where other Sioux were burning and looting the white men's houses. At a narrow bend in the river Joseph waded into the water with Jamie still on his shoulder. On the other side they rested until Joseph was ready to go on. The pale light of dawn had begun to creep into the sky when Joseph knocked at the door of the missionary's cabin.

The fatherly man who opened the door looked tired. "The boy is not harmed," Joseph told him. "His foot is hurt."

Quickly the missionary urged them inside. "God bless you, Joseph," he said. "Bring the boy here with the others." In the kitchen a small group of people sat huddled in blankets near the hearth. There were murmurs of sympathy, and questions buzzed as some of them rose to help.

"You are the bravest Christian we have ever known," the missionary said, taking one of Joseph's hands in his own. "If your people discover what you have done your own life will be in danger. Will you stay here with us now?"

Joseph looked at the faces around him. "Many

others need help. I will go back. Leave the valley and go to the fort while there is still time."

"We will do as you say, Joseph. I would spare you a horse, but you know that we must take them for the wagons." The missionary looked frail and sad.

"I will go as I came," the Indian replied. "It will not be many moons to our Father's house. We shall pass the days in peace then, my friend." As he left, the missionary embraced him and pressed a parcel of food into his hands.

From the blanket where they had laid him, Jamie groaned and closed his eyes. His foot felt like it was on fire. A woman's face bent over him. "You're all right, lad. You're safe now." Gently she examined the swollen foot. "A cold compress will make that feel better."

He tried to sit up, but the pain forced him back. "Joseph?" he called.

"He's gone to help others like us," the woman said.

"Joseph saved my life," he told her. The woman began to cry. For a minute he felt confused. Did she know about his folks? "They're all dead," he whispered, "Ma, Pa, Grandpa and Grandma." Tears spilled down his cheeks as he remembered the burning house and the nightmare sounds.

The woman wrapped her arms around him and held him. "You'll be safe now. You can stay with me till we find your kin. I'm going to Bellfield to live with my brother soon as we can get there," she said softly.

The woman was not much younger than his ma. Her golden hair caught the firelight, and her pale blue eyes shone with tears. To Jamie that first time he saw Miss Ceil she had seemed like an angel.

Even though two years had passed since that night, thinking about it brought a lump to his throat. Jamie brushed the dirt from a root and added it to his pile. Except for Miss Ceil he would have run off from the small prairie town of Bellfield long ago. But how could he leave Miss Ceil alone to slave for her drunken brother, Jory? If she hadn't taken him in after his folks were killed he would have been sent to some county orphan asylum.

In the west the last rays of the setting sun turned the sky pink and gold. Quickly Jamie put the roots he had dug for Miss Ceil into his pouch. He'd been gone too long already.

Hundreds of miles away in New York City Benjamin Stewart Able hastily finished a letter. He scribbled in the date, August 1864, sealed the envelope, and addressed it to his friend Zack at an army post in North Carolina. He handed the envelope to his cousin Abigail. "Thanks," he said, "for mailing this." Now that it was time to leave, Ben couldn't think of what to say. In the year they had been living in New York City with his aunt and uncle, Abigail had shared in a real life-and-death adventure with Zack and Ben. He knew he would miss her.

Abigail's clear blue eyes were serious as she looked at Ben. "I wish we were going with you," she said. "Nothing ever happens in New York

City." She smiled, and then they were laughing hard together. When they stopped she said, "I won't forget you, Ben. Come back someday."

"You know my father," Ben said. "Nothing can keep him from speaking out for the cause of justice. Maybe we won't last long in Minnesota either."

"Your pa is a good man. If those folks in Minnesota can't stand up for a minister who speaks out against slavery, they don't deserve him. Besides, from what I hear they don't have time to think about anything but Indians." Her voice was teasing.

Ben groaned as footsteps sounded on the stairs and someone called his name. "I guess it's time to go," he said. "If I don't get scalped I might be back in a year or two."

He walked slowly to the hall. He didn't want to go. What he wished more than anything was to be in the army with Zack. Already Zack had met another twelve-year-old boy in camp, a drummer boy. Any place would be better than Bellfield, Minnesota.

1

A New Home

Heat lightning flashed across the sky. Ben removed his hat and wiped the sweat from his face. It was hot on the passenger deck of the steamboat. He would rather be down below closer to the muddy waters of the Mississippi and feel the spray as the boat plowed upriver toward Fort Snelling. As they drew nearer to the fort the men on board who had come to join the army crowded the rails for a first sight of it. High above the bluff Ben could see its cannons mounted on gray stone walls.

Ben's mother came to stand by his side at the rail. "We have several hours here before the boat leaves for Bellfield," she said. "I expect you will want to see the fort. Only first do something with that hair of yours." Her gray eyes held a hint of laughter, and Ben smiled. His thick brown hair curled wildly in the hot humid weather. His ran his fingers through it and wiped the sweat from his forehead and the bridge of his nose. He had inherited his father's long straight nose, a trait of most of the Able family men. His mother said softly, "You look so like your father, Ben. Though I believe your eyes are more gray than blue." Ben knew she missed his pa.

While his mother visited with the wives of some of the officers, Ben looked around. He had never seen a fort up close before. Men in blue Union army uniforms were everywhere. In a section of open field he spotted a smartly outfitted drummer boy. He watched as the boy beat out the time for a company of soldiers marching back and forth on the field. For a long while Ben tapped his fingers against a wooden railing in time with the drum. He knew he could learn.

The practice march ended, and the boy walked over to Ben. "Saw you watching," he said. "You planning on joining up?"

"Not yet. My pa says no, but I'm thinking things could change." Ben held out his hand. "Ben Able, here."

The boy shook Ben's hand. "Seth McDougal," he said, "and if you like you can walk back with me to quarters."

Eagerly Ben accepted. "Our boat won't leave for Bellfield for a couple of hours. You from around these parts?"

"From Mankato," Seth answered. "Bellfield is on the Minnesota River not so far from where the Indian uprising was two summers ago, ain't it? General Sibley and his men are still out chasing hostile Sioux that escaped the first round last summer. Your folks will have to be a mite careful if they plan on settling far out from town. Over to Wright County a whole family was killed on their way to a new settlement. Back in Mankato two months ago Indians wiped out one of the farmers." Seth shook his head. "Some of those Indians pass right through our guards, but the general has sworn to hunt down every last one of them." Seth shared his quarters with another drummer boy and two officer's boys who looked to be no more than fifteen. Each of the drummer boys wore woolen caps with brass bugles. "Ain't much," Seth remarked, "but it's home for now. You join up, and the army gives you what you need same as the regular soldiers." One of the other boys laughed and said, "Guess that would be one rubber blanket, two woolen ones, jacket and pants two sizes too large, and the rest of this here stuff you see." Ben smiled as he noted the bedrolls, packs, and personal belongings all carefully stowed as if waiting for inspection.

The other boys were on their way out, and Seth motioned Ben to sit. "Reckon you heard that our troops under General Grant had a big fight with the rebels over the Weldon Railroad no more than four miles from Richmond." Ben knew that rebels was what folks called soldiers who fought in the army of the rebellious South. The South called herself the Confederacy now that she had broken away from being part of the United States rather than give up slavery. But to the Northern states, known as the Union, the Southern states were rebels. The North was at war with the South both to do away with slavery and to prevent the dividing of the United States into two countries. "Looks like half the rebel army is trying to hold off Grant from taking the Peterburg Railroad line to Richmond. The other half of the rebel army is holed up in the Shenandoah Valley waiting for good old General Sheridan to come. Once our troops take over the railroads to Richmond and cut off the food supply from the Shenandoah, this war will be over," Seth said. "I sure hope I get to see some of the action."

"From what I hear," Ben added, "there will be plenty more fighting soon. The papers said General Sherman is moving along the line of rebel defenses looking for a place to turn their position."

The boy nodded. "Heard tell them rebel defense works in Atlanta are fifteen feet high with pretty deep ditches along them. But nothing to fret about. Sherman will find their weak spot. You can count on that," he said knowingly.

Ben stayed until Seth had to leave to drum supper call. Back on board the steamboat Ben strained to catch a final glimpse of Seth and the other boys, but the distance was too great. With a sigh he watched the fort steadily grow smaller as the powerful steam engines moved the boat swiftly up the Minnesota River. The captain was a big man with a weathered face, and a man of great experience on the river. "You won't find a worse river for winding around than this one," he said. "Course, you can't count the Red River, which ain't hardly fit for navigating. Both rivers freeze up five months of the year, and sometimes there ain't enough water in a dry spell to run a big boat on either of them. Leastwise, on the Minnesota a fellow don't meet himself coming around the bend like he does on the Red River. Shouldn't be any grounding this time, thanks to the rain we been having."

True to the captain's word, the Minnesota wound every which way between its thickly wooded banks. Ben wondered how the Red River could be any worse. He figured they had gone around a bend once every mile.

Whatever else Bellfield was like, at least it was on the river where steamboats would be coming and going. Even a town in the middle of nowhere couldn't be too isolated with all that steamboat traffic.

When they were not far from Bellfield the river turned to run beneath a high bluff. A Union soldier on board pointed out the sights. "That's the town of Bellfield on top of that bluff," he said. "She's built on a plain of prairie surrounded by woods. Plenty of oak trees, butternuts, and black cherry in those woods." Turning to Ben he said, "You like strawberries, boy? Up by the schoolhouse there's strawberry patches, and over southeast of town in them hills you can find plenty of wild plums, large yellow ones, mighty good eating. Gallons of berries in Fitzsimmon's woods too, and cranberries in the swamps. Makes my mouth water to think on 'em."

"I guess I'll have no excuse for not putting up preserves," Ben's mother said.

"And, begging your pardon, ma'am, if your husband is a hunting man there's good fat prairie chicken and quail in those woods." His mother smiled and tucked a stray strand of dark hair into her bonnet.

Besides the soldier and themselves there were no other passengers for Bellfield. Ben helped his mother down the boat ramp. She was barely taller than Ben. A few curious folks standing nearby looked their way as he unloaded the last of their boxes.

"Where's Pa?" Ben demanded.

"Your pa will be here." She looked past him, her gray eyes searching. "There he comes!"

Even seated, his father's tall lean frame was unmistakable. A black beaver hat shaded his head. Ben noticed he had on his good preacher's suit.

"Whoa, there." The wagon stopped, and Ben's father jumped down. He lifted Ben's mother off her feet in a great bear hug. Ben grinned at the two small boys who stood nearby staring. Then it was Ben's turn to be smothered in his father's strong arms. "You and your mother have come a long way, son, but you are home now. Minnesota is a good place to live," his father said as he stepped back to look at him.

"I reckon so, Pa," Ben said in a low voice. Minnesota was not home to Ben. He doubted it ever would be, but there was no sense in saying so now.

His father swung their boxes into the back of the wagon and helped Ben's mother up. While the wagon rumbled up the bluff and through the town Ben took note of the wide streets, the three stores, the town hall, and the saloon. On a square by itself was the new frame built church. Beyond the church stood several houses, one of them a large two story house with a wide porch. "That is the judge's house," his father said. "And that one next to it is Deacon Blake's home." He pointed to a white frame house with a large front yard. Behind the house Ben saw an orchard of apple trees loaded with ripening apples. Ben thought he saw the curtains pulled slightly aside in a downstairs window as they passed. He imagined eyes peering at them. Maybe it was a good thing his father had chosen to live on a small farm outside of town.

The wagon bumped along, skirted some holes in the road, and creaked in and out of others. They stopped for a look at the small schoolhouse Ben would attend. It stood in the center of a cleared field bordered in back with tall prairie grasses that stretched to the thick dark woods behind. The one-story frame building looked lonely to Ben.

Outside the town the prairie bloomed with yellow brown-eyed daisies and white and pink flowers in the tall waving grasses. Now and then Ben saw cleared farmland where corn grew taller than the wagon. But as far as he could see, the land was mostly prairie reaching to the very edge of dark green forests. "Ben, you and your mother will like the folks here," his father said. "It's a struggling church, Sarah, but the folks are friendly and eager to meet you both. They've planned a welcome social tomorrow afternoon."

Ben clenched his fingers more tightly to the wagon's sides. He was not ready for a social yet. It didn't make sense for city folks like his father to take on a country church way out in the middle of nowhere. Why couldn't they have stayed in New York?

His father turned the wagon down a narrow path between a stand of butternut trees. In front of them stood a log cabin. Red checked curtains hung in the windows. At the corner of the cabin Ben could see part of the kitchen garden out back, a cornfield, and beyond that the tall prairie grasses edging to the woods.

His father stopped the horse. "It isn't what I'd hoped to bring you to, Sarah, for your first winter in Minnesota." His voice was quiet. "But she's snug and tight."

"Oh, Stewart," she cried. Her voice broke, and tears filled her eyes.

His father looked worried. "It's only temporary, Sarah. We can manage this year and build a frame house next spring."

Ben's mother sniffed. "Silly," she cried. "This isn't the first little place we've called home. I'm just so touched by the flower boxes." She pointed. "Look, Ben; who ever saw a log cabin with flower boxes at the windows?"

Ben's father smiled broadly as his wife stepped down from the wagon and ran to examine the pink petunias and yellow marigolds filling the wooden boxes he had nailed to the log frame.

"Go on, son, walk around. Get a feel for the place

while I show your mother what the good folks of Bellfield sent over to stock her pantry."

Ben felt like he'd already seen it all. Except for the few farms dotted here and there, what else was there in Bellfield? He sauntered toward the small barn that stood out back near a cluster of sheds, one of them the outhouse.

He poked his head into the barn. It smelled like old hay and felt cool. Out in the garden he bent to examine an odd-shaped stone. Its edges were notched, and the shape of it was definitely an arrowhead. Indians—around here? Carefully he wiped it off and stuck it into his pocket. Suddenly the tall prairie grass, the woods, even the cornfield looked as if they might hide anything. Ben walked slowly toward the house, searching the horizon as he walked.

Above the two-room cabin was a sleeping loft for Ben's bed and a ladder to reach it. In the large room that served as kitchen and living room, supper waited on the table. As Ben took his place he held the arrowhead out to his father. "I found this out back."

His father examined it closely. "The Indians were here a long time before the settlers. There is no telling how old this could be."

"Didn't you say, Pa, that Bellfield wasn't attacked in that Sioux Indian uprising two years ago? Guess it couldn't be from then, could it?"

"Bellfield was not raided," his father said. "Refugees from towns farther downriver southwest of

Bellfield fled here to safety. Some of them never went back to what was left of their homes." He shook his head sadly. "More than five hundred settlers were killed during the attacks. Minnesota will be a long time healing from those wounds. That's one of the reasons we came here, son. Bellfield hasn't had a pastor for two years now."

"What happened to the last pastor?" Ben asked.

"With both an Indian war going on in Minnesota and the Civil War at the same time, any man who could help was needed. Pastor Wilson volunteered. He died in the Indian attack at New Ulm."

Ben thought of what Seth had told him about Indians attacking lonely settlements. He knew the army had moved the Sioux tribe out of Minnesota to a reservation in Nebraska Territory. Hundreds of Indians had been sent to prison after the uprising, and thirty-eight were hung on the same day. "Guess the army is still hunting for hostile Sioux." At least Ben hoped they were.

Ben's mother said thoughtfully, "There is another side to this sad affair, Ben. Not all of the Sioux Indians were guilty of crimes. But all of them have been made to suffer for the crimes of their tribesmen. Even the women and children and the elderly are suffering. If you and I were Sioux Indians right now we could be starving and sick, barely able to keep alive on that wretched barren land in Nebraska. The army keeps them penned in like animals with no hope of going back to their homes."

Ben's hand closed carefully over the arrowhead. "That isn't fair," he said.

"No. It's not," his mother stated firmly.

"Not everyone feels like your mother does, Ben," Pa said. "I wish they did, but the men who want the Indians' land have an excuse now. Feelings run deep here in Bellfield against the Indians. We must do all we can to bring about justice and peace."

Ben opened his hand and looked at the arrowhead. Peace? Maybe. But if his father stood up for the Indians, trouble would surely follow. He wished they had stayed in New York where at least he knew somebody.

At nine o'clock it was still light outside, and Ben stood watching a flock of pigeons so thick it looked like a cloud flying overhead. He felt lonely, like a bird who had been left behind. If only he had run off to the war with Zack when he had the chance.

Beyond the cornfield the tall swaying prairie grasses whispered as if they held secrets. A sudden movement that caught Ben's eye startled him. A fat brown gopher darted out of the cornfield then back again. Ben listened for another movement, but all he could hear was his own heart beating loudly. He waited for a few seconds then went inside.

In the shadows a redheaded boy bent low between the cornstalks and carefully backed away from the gopher hole he had disturbed.

2

The Beating

Ben pushed open the schoolhouse door. The single large room seemed full of chattering, restless boys and girls already seated on benches behind long wooden planks that served as desks. He had not intended to be late, especially this first morning. Not sure what he was supposed to do, he stood still for a moment. At the front of the room, Schoolmaster Bron, the man who had introduced himself as the teacher at the church picnic, had his back turned to the class. Yesterday, though Ben had seen him only for a minute, he had thought his manner cool, almost unfriendly.

As Ben searched for an empty desk, Mr. Bron turned and glared at him. "I do not tolerate lateness, even from the preacher's son." His voice was cold and hard. "I shall not punish you this time, but take care in the future. You may be seated next to the gentleman on your left."

Half aware of what he was doing, Ben stumbled into the empty seat next to a stout boy with straw-colored hair. The boy grinned slyly at him and shoved his slate into Ben's arm as soon as the teacher's back was turned. Before Ben could say a thing, the schoolroom door opened once more.

A slightly built boy of about Ben's age, with a mop of red hair, sauntered into the room. Ben noted the boy's ragged shirt and pants, his bare feet, and the look of defiance on his face as he slid into a seat next to one of the girls.

Mr. Bron waited till the boy was seated. "You, sir, James Hill, are late." Mr. Bron's dark eyes glittered, a kind of fierce look of triumph in them. "Come here, sir," he commanded.

The boy rose from his seat slowly and walked steadily to the front of the room. Without waiting to be told, he held out his hands palms up.

"It is commonly held that red hair is a sign of a stubborn nature," the schoolmaster said sternly. "I have suspected such a nature in you, sir, from the beginning. As an orphan you must learn to submit to authority. I will do my utmost to teach you, sir. Thomas Wickens, come here and get down on your hands and knees so that Master James can lean upon your solid back for his whipping." A terrible stillness had come over the room. The stout boy next to Ben hurriedly left his seat and made his way to the front. Awkwardly he knelt down and braced his hands on the floor in front of him.

From his desk Mr. Bron produced a cane. Ben turned his eyes away as the boy called James leaned over his live whipping post. Seven times Ben heard the swish of air and the thwack of the cane's impact on the boy's back. When it was over both boys were sent to their seats.

"Serves him right, the little beggar," the stout boy whispered. Ben felt a flush of anger and pretended not to hear. Back home in New York, a whipping was not something you got for being late. In fact, he couldn't remember anything like this one. Most of his teachers were the kind who made you stay after school or do extra work. The worst he remembered was two whacks across the knuckles for fighting on the playground. Something about Mr. Bron made Ben nervous. It was more than just the way he had called him the preacher's son.

During the reading lesson Mr. Bron called Ben's name. "You, sir, Benjamin Able, let us hear you read."

Ben stood to his feet and read from the book that the older students were using. Reading was one of his best subjects, and he read easily. He had read one paragraph when Mr. Bron interrupted him.

"We should like to hear a little more enthusiasm next time, sir. Sit down."

Ben's face burned as he sat, and Mr. Bron called on someone else. This time it was a girl who read as if she were trying out for the part of the angel Gabriel in a Christmas play. For several minutes she read on.

"Thank you, Miss Blake. You may be seated," Mr. Bron said with a nod of his head. Ben noted the flush of pleasure on the girl's face.

At the noon recess, some of the boys gathered to

watch a game of marbles. Most of the girls clus-
tered together on the far side of the field, and the
younger children ran to play their games under a
nearby oak tree. Ben watched the marbles game for
a while, then walked along the edge of the field
where the waist-high grasses bordered it. He spotted the boy Jamie propped on one elbow, reclining
on his side in the grass and chewing a stem of
clover.

"Hi," Ben said. "Looks like a good place to sit."

The boy's head turned toward him. "Help yourself. It's a free country," he said.

Ben sat down. "I don't think I saw you at the
church picnic yesterday."

"You're new around these parts," the boy replied.
"The name's Jamie Hill, as you may already have
heard."

Ben nodded his head. "I heard. I'm Ben Able, the
preacher's son, as the whole school heard." The boy
laughed, and Ben laughed with him. "Is Bron always
like that?" Ben asked.

"He came last year after the regular teacher, Miss
Lamer, had to leave midterm to take care of the
young ones when their ma died back east. I guess
the town was glad to get anybody they could."
Jamie was silent for a moment. "I reckon he has
his likes and his dislikes. Just so happens I'm one
of his dislikes."

"I didn't pick up he was too keen on ministers'
kids either," Ben said. "You took a mighty big lick-

ing for being late. Don't know if I would have stood it like you did."

"You would if you had to. Leastwise he doesn't hold a candle to Old Man Jory once the whiskey gets in him," Jamie said.

"I hope this Jory fellow isn't a substitute teacher or something," Ben said fervently.

When Jamie smiled his whole face got involved, as it did now, crinkling his eyes and moving his freckles. It reminded Ben a little of his father's smile.

"Old Jory couldn't read his own name," Jamie said. "He's not my pa or anything, just the guardian I have to put up with till I'm out of here."

"Whiskey can make some folks pretty mean. I knew a fellow back in New York whose pa nearly beat him to death before he ran away. Last I heard, he was planning on coming west," Ben said.

Jamie laughed. "Well, if he does, I hope he has better luck than some. Jory's a bad one. If it wasn't for Miss Ceil, I'd have lit out long ago. She's his sister and only living relative, but the two of them are as different as a ferret from an otter." Jamie sat up.

Ben wanted to go on talking, but the warning bell that recess was over sounded loud and clear. "Guess it won't do to be late," he said.

The boy winced as he stood to his feet. "Wouldn't do at all," he said and grinned. Together they hurried toward the others milling into the school-house.

When Ben slid into his seat the stout boy who

had been Jamie's whipping post was already seated. He looked at Ben with a serious expression. "You don't want to mix with the likes of him if you know what's good for you." Jamie had just passed their row on his way to his own desk. "Trash, that's what," the boy said. "He ain't from around here. Came here an orphan to live with that old drunk Jory. He's got red hair like a lot of them Irish immigrants. They're all drinkers, the lot of them. Bet he's one of them."

"Who says?" Ben whispered fiercely.

"My pa, that's who. My pa don't hold to drinking. No Wickens is gonna mix with that Irish trash," Thomas Wickens whispered back just as fiercely.

A sharp rap of Mr. Bron's cane brought the room to the stillness of stone. For the rest of the afternoon lesson followed lesson without a break. Ben had little time to think about anything else though he couldn't help but notice Mr. Bron's cane. Once it tapped sharply on the desk directly in front of Ben. In between times it kept a kind of rhythmic rapping against the side of Mr. Bron's leather boot, a sort of soft snakelike warning of its presence.

School was dismissed, and Mr. Bron stood at the door as each student passed in front of him. Ben kept his eyes focused straight ahead. He was unprepared for the light tap of the cane on his shoulder.

"Benjamin Able, I trust you will remember that we begin school on time?" Though it was a kind of question, Mr. Bron spoke the words so that they hissed a warning Ben couldn't miss.

"Yes, sir," Ben said quietly without looking at the man.

Outside in the sunshine Ben breathed deeply as though even the air here was somehow less dangerous than inside the schoolroom.

For a while he walked alongside Thomas Wickens and three other boys: Sam Banks, a tall lanky farm boy; Lucas Teachman, a boy with a heavily pockmarked face; and Will Coster, a short broad-shouldered lad with a ready smile. Jamie Hill was nowhere in sight when Ben glanced around for him.

Out of sight of the schoolhouse three of the girls had stopped to pick berries. As the boys reached them Thomas swooped up a lunch pail and raced off with it toward the woods.

The youngest girl, a child of about eight, started running after him. "You come back here," she cried. Lucas and Sam snatched up the lunch pails of the other girls as they ran to help their friend. The boys raced past the girls by zigging and zagging out of their reach and ran on toward the stream that meandered near the path.

By the time Ben and Will caught up with the girls, the lunch pails were lying in the shallow stream. Thomas, Lucas, and Sam, hooting and laughing, waved their hands as they disappeared around a bend in the path.

"You mean, lower-than-a-skunk tormentors!" The girl who had read in class right after him faced

Ben, her two hands clenched tightly into fists. Her black eyes flashed.

"Whoa there," Ben said quickly. "I'm not the one you ought to be mad at." Without waiting for an answer Ben waded into the stream and rescued the lunch pails. He set the water-filled pails on the ground and stepped back. "There you go. Better get them dry pretty quick."

The third girl stared at Ben, her clear blue eyes uncertain. Then quickly she bent down and picked up one of the pails. "Thanks," she murmured.

Ben smiled and was about to say something when the one with flashing eyes scooped up her pail and emptied its contents all over Ben.

"What did I do?" Ben said indignantly.

She made no reply other than what sounded like "Humph!" as she picked up the other pail and handed it to the youngest girl. Quickly she turned away, her long dark braids flapping against her back as she dragged the small girl with her.

"Wait for me, Tess," the blond one said as she followed the others.

Ben's shoes were wet, and now the rest of him dripped water. Angrily he wiped at his face. "Girls. Who needs them?" he said.

Will, who had been almost as taken aback as Ben, grinned and shook his head. "Looks like a fellow can't do right nohow when it comes to Tessie Blake. Come on. You can dry off at our back porch just up a ways. Grandpa will be glad to see company. He was mighty glad when your pa got here."

Ben's shoes squished with water. He bent to remove them. Maybe it wouldn't hurt to go by Will's place for a little while. He was curious to see where Will lived. And this was the first invitation from a new schoolmate. "Sounds good to me," Ben said.

The cool damp of the earth felt good on Ben's bare feet. Will too had removed his shoes and slung them by the laces across his shoulder. As they walked on the hard packed path Ben thought of Jamie Hill and like a flash remembered that Jamie hadn't worn shoes to school. Casually he said, "I didn't see Jamie Hill when school let out. I reckon he must live somewhere on the other side of town."

"Old Man Jory keeps a place at the edge of Bethel Woods. You'd best not go 'round there. He's meaner than an old billy goat. He'd sic the dogs on you soon as you set foot on his property." Will stooped to pick up an acorn and sent it skipping ahead of them. "Likes his own company, that one. I mean Jamie Hill. Keeps to himself mostly. Grandpa says that's because he lost his folks in the Indian uprising and ain't got over it yet." Will paused. "You sure got to admire his grit. That ain't the first time Bron has caned him."

"Is Bron that mean all the time?" Ben asked.

Will pressed his lips together then slowly nodded. "I reckon he don't change much. So long as you keep out of sight and don't cross him he's tolerable."

Ben didn't think much of Will's answer.

3

A Reason to Stay

Deep in the woods where the stream ran freely over a rocky bottom, a flash of red hair disappeared as Jamie drew his bloodstained shirt away from his back and over his head. With a groan he quickly removed his trousers and lowered himself belly down into the cold stream. In a moment he raised his head above the shallow water. The icy water stung at first but quickly brought a soothing numbness to his raw back. It was unfair that he'd been whipped for doing right. Miss Ceil's cough was so bad she couldn't tend to her usual chores, and Jamie had done them for her as well as his own before leaving for school. Tears of anger ran down his face.

Alone in the woods he let himself cry. Why him? Why did his ma and pa have to go and die? Worse, why didn't God just take him, too, instead of letting old Joseph rescue him? The thought of the Indian Joseph who had been a true friend brought fresh tears to his eyes. Joseph had been put in prison along with other Indians after the uprising. Miss Ceil had gone to testify for him, but before she arrived Joseph had already been hung by mistake.

The sad, still pretty face of Miss Ceil rose in his mind. She feared her own brother and his whiskey rages. Jory was plain evil. Gingerly, Jamie raised himself and left the stream. For her sake he would stay on, for a while anyway, but as soon as he was sure she was safe he would run away. He gathered up his clothes and dressed, wincing as the rough material of the shirt touched his back.

The dogs were nowhere in sight when Jamie approached the leaning rail fence around the farmhouse. The house had been built for Jory's new bride, Miss Ceil said, but the young woman died before she could live in it. Jory buried his bride in a little clearing in the woods back of the house. Miss Ceil said that the tragedy was what turned her brother the way he was now. Anyway, for the moment the dogs were gone, and that meant Jory was out, probably off hunting.

Miss Ceil was fixing supper when Jamie walked in. She searched his face with her large dark eyes made larger by the deep circles under them. "You okay?" she asked. "I hope you weren't late to school. After you did all the work this morning I just stayed in bed most of the day. I feel lots better tonight, thanks to you."

Jamie nodded. He had scrubbed his shirt carefully to get out the tell-tale stains. She would only worry if she knew he'd been caned again by Bron.

Even with her yellow hair pulled back in a bun, she looked like a young girl in the dress and apron that hung on her thin frame. "We might as well eat," she said. "No telling when Jory will be back."

With just the two of them at the kitchen table it was almost as if Jory didn't exist. Jamie ate his stew hungrily. Miss Ceil could make almost anything taste good, that is, when Jory wasn't around. The two of them had gone to bed supperless many a night when Jory in a drunken rage filled the kitchen with broken crockery. Once Miss Ceil had locked herself and Jamie into the cellar till Jory fell asleep.

Miss Ceil sat down across from him at the table. "Jamie, I've been thinking. It doesn't seem right for you to go on living here with Jory the way he is. I mean, I'm his sister and all, but you have your whole life ahead of you." Her voice was urgent. "For all we know, there's kin of yours somewhere out there who'd be glad to welcome their own." She turned her pale face away for a moment, but not before Jamie had caught the glint of tears in her eyes. "Besides, what will you do if something should happen to me?" Quickly she looked back at him. "I mean, what with the winter coming on. I don't know, Jamie, if I'd last another sickness like last winter's."

Jamie shook his head. "You heard what Doc Bruder said. If ever you feel poorly he wants you to go to him right away and not wait so long. I'm not leaving you here with Jory. Anyway, I ain't got kin. None that I know about. I reckon there's just you." He smiled at her, trying not to let her see the ache he felt inside.

"Jamie, you're like my own little brother. It's just that I'm worried what Jory would do in one of his drunk rages and nobody here to help you."

"You got to stop thinking like that. I'm right pleased to be brother to you, but no way am I any kin of Jory's. Sorry if that makes you feel bad. I just can't help myself." Jamie looked away half ashamed.

"I understand, Jamie. Still I can't help worrying."

"Listen, Miss Ceil. I've been thinking some too. The big fair is coming soon as the farmers get the harvesting finished. It's to help our soldiers, ain't it?" Jamie leaned forward, his eyes intent. "And Luke Henry will surely be there now that his leg's healed. He don't even limp much lately. And I know he's sweet on you. Was before he went off to war and got himself wounded at Gettysburg."

Miss Ceil blushed and looked down at the table. "What are you thinking?" she said so softly Jamie barely caught the words.

In his earnestness Jamie grasped her hand in one of his own. "You got to go. Luke Henry's a good man, even if he don't deserve you, Miss Ceil. He'd take care of you. I know he would."

"Oh, Jamie, even if Luke Henry did care, my brother would never let me go without a fuss. You know he won't let anyone come round here, not even folks from the church. Don't fret, Jamie. I was happy with my Michael, and I'll always be grateful for the time we had together." She brushed away tears and picked up Jamie's empty plate.

"Luke Henry's not the one to let even Jory stand in his way," Jamie said. "Promise you'll go no matter what Jory says. I bet nobody can make a better apple pie than you can, Miss Ceil, and I know where there's a whole tree of wild ones waiting to be picked. They are sour enough now to turn a fellow's mouth green, but you know it just takes a few weeks of setting around to mellow them. If I pick them now they'll be ready for the fair. And it just happens Mr. Dolan says he needs all the ginseng root I can bring him." Mr. Dolan owned the town's one general store. "That means I can trade for flour and sugar." He grinned impishly at her.

"You are persistent, Master James. I suppose I do owe it to the war effort to take something to the sale. Mind you, pick me plenty apples then, and good ones." As she cleared the wooden table of the supper things she said, "I'll tell Jory myself when the time comes."

Jamie tried to picture Miss Ceil at the fair. He had pretended not to notice when Miss Ceil's Sunday dress became so worn even she couldn't patch it. Her second best would do for the social, he thought. It still had a pretty collar and a bit of lace at the sleeves. Besides, Luke Henry never took his eyes off her face.

Jamie's steps were almost light as he went to fetch more wood for the stove. He lifted a last piece onto his load. In the distance a dog barked, then another. Jory. Quickly Jamie headed for the kitchen and deposited the wood. One hasty glance out the kitchen window showed Jory weaving from one side of the path to the other. In a few minutes Jamie heard his heavy boots stumbling onto the porch. He beat a hasty retreat upstairs. Usually when Jory was like this he did not bother to climb the steep staircase but fell asleep on the parlor sofa till morning. If he didn't fall asleep he would most likely come looking for Jamie, and that meant trouble.

At the door of her bedroom Miss Ceil stood white-faced, her eyes questioning. Jamie nodded, and quickly she stepped aside for him to enter. He shut the door behind him. Together they moved a heavy chest against the door. Jamie would sleep on the floor tonight. It was safer that way.

While Miss Ceil put down a quilt for him, Jamie checked the window. He had made a crude rope ladder for them, in case of things like a fire, and fastened it to the bedstead. Satisfied, he plunked himself down on the floor.

Miss Ceil handed Jamie the small Bible she kept on her nightstand. Carefully she moved the lamp so that it shone down on him. "The marker's at the place we stopped last time," she said softly.

Jamie turned the pages to where the marker stuck out. "Psalm 23," he read. "The Lord is my shepherd." He glanced up at her. "That the one?" he asked.

"That's it, Jamie. The very one. Read it for us, please."

In the lamplight her golden hair shone, and her blue eyes glistened with tears. In spite of the dark circles under her eyes, her face wore a gentle, kind look.

To Jamie she still looked like an angel. In a hushed voice he read the words he knew she loved to hear. Downstairs a sudden crash startled them both. For a minute he stopped reading to listen. In a moment they heard Jory moving about, and Jamie continued to read.

4

A Letter from Zack

In front of Will's cabin three older ladies sat in wooden chairs working on a quilt. "Those are my aunts," Will said. "They been living with us since the Indian uprising. Scared to go anywhere now. They used to live with my uncle in New Ulm. After he was killed in the raids they came here. Never did go back to New Ulm. They don't like to hear the word *Indian* mentioned."

Secretly Ben hoped the old ladies wouldn't come to church. He knew his pa would mention Indians sooner or later.

When it was time to leave, Will showed Ben a shortcut. It was an easy path through the woods and came out just below the butternut trees near the cabin. The wagon stood nearby. That meant his father was already home.

Ben's mother looked up from the letter in her hands, a question in her eyes. His father, seated at the kitchen table with a stack of books in front of him, smiled and beckoned him to come.

"Not so fast, young man," his mother said. "What on earth have you been doing? You've left a trail of muddy footprints all over the oilcloth."

Ben glanced behind him at the dark red oilcloth on the kitchen floor and remembered his wet shoes. "Sorry," he said retreating to the cabin door to remove them. The oilcloth was his mother's pride. As he wiped mud from the floor he tried to explain about the girls and the lunch pails.

"Well, now, you might have used a stick to fish the pails out instead of filling your own good shoes," his mother said.

Ben wondered why he hadn't thought of that. How silly he must have looked jumping into a stream with his shoes on. The whole school would probably know about it by tomorrow. The thought made him cringe.

"Sarah, did I ever tell you about my first day at a new school when I was about Ben's age?" his father asked and laughed. "Long before the rest of the household was up I was dressed and ready to go. It was not until recess that I happened to glance down at my feet and notice one brown stocking and one black one." Ben smiled, and his mother laughed.

"By the way, Ben, this came today. I expect it's from Zack." The letter his father held looked official.

Ben nearly tipped over a chair in his dash for the letter. At the top of the thin paper was an eagle and the American flag with the words *One Country, One Destiny*, and underneath, *The United States Sanitary Commission*. The Sanitary Commission was an organization that provided many services for the armed forces during the war. Ben read on.

He was used to Zack's carefully formed letters, his plain way of writing. Aloud he read:

"Things are sure different since Chaplain Turner got smallpox. The officer in charge makes us step mighty lively. It's hard on some of the sick men who can't get back on their feet on account of they have to report for duty sick or not. Chaplain Turner will set things right when he gets back I told the men.

"We still need spelling books as many of the men want to learn and there are not too many books. I teach some of the boys for an hour before we turn in for the night, but we keep a watch out since the new officer don't hold with colored men doing book learning.

"I sure do thank your ma for the cookies she sent from New York. I spent a lot of time guarding them from the rest of the company.

"I feel fine. The food ain't like home, but the coffee sure is good."

Ben paused to add, "He never liked coffee much before."

He read on: "The new officer says I need to help the cook. I don't mind, but I'll be glad when Chaplain Turner comes back.

The men here can't hardly wait till we move out. Ben, you ain't seen nothing like Chaplain Turner's horse. This morning I got to walk him. He's a fiery one, but we did just fine."

Ben looked up and smiled. One thing about Zack was certain. He had a way with horses. Even the most skittish seemed to cotton to Zack.

"You take care of yourself, Ben. Can't say when I'll be getting out west. You tell your ma and pa thank you for me. I can't think of anything better than seeing you all. Don't go forgetting me, Ben.

Yours truly,
Zack"

Ben's father nodded. "It sounds like Zack is doing well. I hope Chaplain Turner will be well enough to return to his men soon. Smallpox is serious, but the chaplain is a strong man. He is a good man, a chaplain to his own people, and a fine example for Zack."

Hope filled Ben's insides as he looked earnestly at his father. "Pa, I want to join up. Will said he heard about a white drummer boy my age marching with one of the regiments. I know I could do it, Pa, please."

His mother's gray eyes were fearful, her face anxious. "You don't know anything about war, son, and I don't want you learning while you're still a schoolboy," she said firmly.

"But Ma, what about that drummer boy my age? The papers say that the South can't hold out much longer. It wouldn't be for long," Ben pleaded.

"That's enough, Ben," his father said. "The fact that the war may be coming to an end just adds to the point: there's no good reason why you should go. In the first place, one underage drummer boy doesn't mean the army is in the habit of hiring schoolboys. And if it hadn't been for Chaplain Turner, Zack most likely wouldn't be with the First

Colored Regiment. I doubt the chaplain will be letting Zack too near any battles. In the second place, you've a responsibility to your schooling right now." His father lowered his voice. "May the day never come when you are forced to go to war. But should that time come, you will be ready for it, son. Meanwhile, I suggest you put your mind to the tasks at hand."

Ben felt his face flush. School. Everything centered on school. With as much control as he could muster, he met his father's eyes. "Yes, sir," he said. With Zack's letter in his hand he walked slowly toward the door.

"Clean up those shoes, Ben, before you come back in," his mother called behind him.

Ben headed for the barn. Inside its cool, quiet, musty smelling walls he slumped down against a post. School. Already he hated the thought of facing that man Bron and his cane. Any place would be better than here. Zack was the lucky one.

He wanted to tell his father about Bron, about the licking Jamie had taken, but Zack's letter had changed things. He couldn't tell his folks now. If they wouldn't let him join up because he was a schoolboy, his complaints about school would only make them say that going off to war would be harder. He would just have to keep it to himself and try to stay out of Bron's way.

Slowly he read Zack's letter again. Here and there the paper was smudged with what looked like mud. Zack wouldn't care about a little mud, and neither would he. They had been through plenty of hard places together. For the first time since Zack had run off to the army Ben felt an overwhelming loneliness.

Even if Zack came to Bellfield, how long would he stay? There were no blacks in any of the classes in school. Bron might make fierce trouble for both Zack and him if he took a mind to it.

Zack's letters sounded like the same old Zack. But things change. Zack was drinking coffee now and liking it. That wasn't anything, but just the same, it gave Ben a funny feeling of being left behind. Ben looked at the old pile of hay near his feet. Maybe he would not stay behind next time. When Zack came for a visit Ben would find a way to leave with him. He kicked at the hay.

A tiny ladybug scurried by his boot. Ben watched it climb a wisp of straw. Carefully he picked it up, carried it outside, and shook the bug off the straw onto a bed of flowers. "Don't you know God didn't make ladybugs to live in a barn?" he said aloud. "And he didn't make me to live in Bellfield, Minnesota, or go to Bron's school, either."

Back at the cabin doorway his mother stood watching Ben. She leaned against the door frame; her gray eyes were sad. As Ben's father joined her she took his arm with one slender hand but said nothing.

"The boy will be fine. Give him time, Sarah," he urged. "It will take a while to put his roots down. It isn't home for him yet, not yet."

Ben's mother wiped her eyes with the end of her apron. "I know, dear. And with school started things should get better. He'll be making new friends and learning new things." Thinking of the school she sighed with relief and patted her husband's arm.

She didn't see Ben pick up a long, cane-like stick and break it into dozens of little pieces till there was nothing left. Tomorrow he would make a point of finding out exactly where at the edge of Bethel Woods Jamie Hill lived. At least the two of them had something in common. No one could call them favorites of Mr. Bron!

For a minute he thought about the man called Jory and his dogs. Well, he didn't own the woods. Ben would keep a safe distance if he could. All the same, he was going. There was something about Jamie Hill that reminded him of another boy, a spunky orphan who had helped Ben and Zack out of a real jam back in New York.

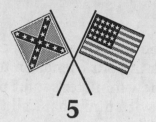

5

An Unexpected Rival

Ben slowed his steps as he neared the oak by the path to Jamie's place. Tucked in the branches was a bit of white cloth. The boys had agreed on a signal. A white rag in the oak by the path meant Jory was out and Ben could come, a black one meant go back. Jamie was not allowed visitors. Will Coster was right; nobody went near Jory's place if they could help it. The man was plain mean. Fortunately he liked to hunt and sometimes would be gone with the dogs for two days at a time. The signal worked well. So far he hadn't run into old Jory once. Ben was totally unprepared for what happened next.

"Morning," Jamie said, as he came down the path to the oak.

His red hair was still wet where he had slicked it down for school. Ben was about to answer when a figure stepped from behind a nearby thicket. Jamie's face paled. "Didn't expect you, Jory," he said quickly.

The thin-shouldered, bearded man stepped closer and suddenly gripped Jamie's shoulder. "So that's your game. You wait till you think I ain't around so you can sneak in your friends on to my property."

"Ben's the new minister's son. I planned on walking to school with him, that's all," Jamie said. His voice was steady and he looked straight into Jory's eyes as he spoke.

Jory narrowed his dark eyes and stared at Ben. "I reckon he's big enough to find his own way to school." Then he turned once more to Jamie. Ben saw as the man's hand squeezed Jamie's shoulder hard. "You get on to school, you hear? I'll be waiting for you when you come back. Ain't nobody setting foot on this property without my say, you hear, boy?"

"I hear you," Jamie replied. With a shove Jory released his hold on Jamie, and without another word he strode toward the house. As they hurried away Jamie muttered, "He must have seen the white cloth and figured something was up. He is meaner than a pole cat."

"We'll have to meet further up the path on school mornings," Ben said. "There ain't any sense taking chances with a man like that. I suppose he will be waiting for you like he said. It makes me mad."

"It won't be the first time. I just keep telling myself that as soon as Miss Ceil is out of here, I'm going," Jamie said. "After the fair, things might take a turn for the better. You planning to go the fair?"

Ben nodded. "Guess so. My ma's been making her special crab apple-apple jelly. You going?"

"You bet. I got to see Miss Ceil gets there with her pies. And Luke Henry had better be there too. He's sweet on Miss Ceil. I aim to see that he gets a chance to court her."

Ben grinned. "Didn't know you played Cupid."

"Got my reasons," Jamie retorted. "Once Miss Ceil's safe with a good man like Luke Henry to take care of her, I'm off."

Ben nodded. He knew it was true. Jamie stayed only because of Miss Ceil.

In the school yard a group of girls stood close together talking and laughing. One of them was Tessie Blake. As Ben and Jamie approached she turned away so that her back was to Ben.

"Now, what's the matter with her?" Ben said softly.

"Couldn't say," Jamie said, "unless it's because today's the big spelling bee and she knows you're her only real rival."

"Oh, no," Ben moaned. "Not again." Why did it have to be a girl, especially Tessie Blake? It seemed as if the two of them were always competing. Ben had scored highest in math and Tessie second highest, but she had won in geography.

"The Blakes are the upper class around here," Jamie pointed out. "Mr. Blake owns a lot of property and railroad rights. I hear he's even invested in a mine up north. He's a deacon at the church too. If that ain't enough, Mrs. Blake comes from monied people back east."

Ben didn't answer him. He glanced at Tessie.

Why did she dislike him so much? The only thing he could think of was the day he'd rescued her lunch pail. Did she blame him because he was walking with the other fellows who had stolen them?

Aloud he said, "All I know is that Tessie Blake can't stand losing, and Bron will probably make me out a fool in front of the class if he can."

"Don't you let him get to you," Jamie commanded fiercely as the warning bell rang.

The spelling bee came late in the morning. One by one the boys on Ben's side of the room took their seats. There were still two girls standing, Tessie Blake and her blond friend Hilda Loos. Hilda stumbled on the word *demagogue*, and only Tessie remained facing Ben. She held her chin high and refused to look at Ben.

"Master Able, you will kindly spell the word *puerile*, sir."

Ben faltered for a second. It was a word unfamiliar to him. Slowly he spelled out the sounds: *"p-u-r-i-l-e."*

Mr. Bron turned to Tessie. "Master Able was close but incorrect. Perhaps you will do better, Miss Blake."

Without hesitating Tessie spelled *"p-u-e-r-i-l-e."*

"Excellent," Mr. Bron said. "Miss Blake has won our spelling bee. You may return to your seats." He nodded briefly in Ben's direction. "The word, sir, means foolish, and if you knew your Latin or your French you might know that."

Ben went back to his desk, his face hot with anger. Bron had it in for him, no matter what Ben did—right or wrong. Thomas Wickens grinned at him as he sat down. "Didn't they teach you that in New York?"

The schoolmaster rapped for attention. "As you know, class, the fair to benefit our soldiers is only two weeks away. This afternoon instead of our usual studies we are invited guests at Mr. and Mrs. Blake's home to help do our share in the preparations." Excited murmurs and whispers rose in the room, and Mr. Bron tapped sharply with his cane. "Silence. We must conduct ourselves as ladies and gentlemen. Mr. Blake's orchards are large, and as you know, due to the war there is a shortage of farmhands in Bellfield. You will help gather windfalls, the apples knocked down by yesterday's high winds. I understand that there will be refreshments for all. Those of you who brought lunches may bring them. We shall leave at once."

On their way to line up in the school yard, Tessie had passed Ben with a toss of her black braid and her chin high in the air. At the back of the line Jamie marched behind Ben. "Maybe you ought to be glad about now that you didn't win over Miss Blake. Think what it would be like at her place this afternoon if you had," Jamie said.

"She can't stand the sight of me, noways," Ben said. "I reckon my losing won't make any difference."

Mrs. Blake and several ladies from the church were busily setting tables in the yard. Mrs. Blake wore a blue gingham dress and a spotless white apron as she passed platters of apple cake and fried cakes. Hilda's mother served ice cold buttermilk. Those who had brought lunches either left them unopened or stuffed them in quickly between apple cake and fried cakes.

On his third fried cake, Jamie smacked his lips. "One thing you've got to admit, Tessie's ma sure knows how to make fried cakes."

"Why thank you, James," Mrs. Blake said, coming around the tree Ben and Jamie were leaning against. "You must have another, dear. You too, Benjamin."

Jamie colored. "I don't mind if I do, ma'am. They surely are good."

Ben took another and thanked Mrs. Blake, who hurried off toward a group of girls deep in conversation with Hilda and Tessie.

Gathering the windfalls was easy enough, except that there were a lot more of them than Ben had imagined. "How come they just don't pick them all?" Ben asked Jamie, who was working under the same tree. "Looks to me like the ones still on the trees are red enough."

Jamie answered without stopping his work. "Farmers around here say that the best apples are the ones after the first good frost. Ought to be one any time now."

Ben picked up an apple then dropped it quickly. "Ugh! Full of worms, that one."

"Don't matter none," Jamie said. "You just throw it all into the cider pot and presto, no worms."

"That's rotten," Ben observed and secretly vowed never to drink cider at Jamie's place. He ignored the bad apple and went on picking up the others gingerly. By the end of the school day he no longer stopped to inspect the underside of the apples he tossed into his bag. Probably somebody inspected the ones that went into the cider. At least he hoped so.

Mr. Bron stood by the large barrels of apples talking to Mr. Blake as Ben and Jamie approached to dump their last load of apples. "Guess you can expect a few more pupils when our orphans from New York City arrive. Quite proper of Reverend Able to volunteer Bellfield homes for them. What with so many of our men folk gone off to war our farmers can use any help they can get. Orphans need to learn to work hard, earn their keep," Mr. Blake was saying. "Like the Bible says, if a man won't work, don't let him eat. A little sweat of the brow never hurt anyone, eh?"

"I have indeed found it so, sir," Mr. Bron agreed. "You may rest assured they will work hard in my school. I shall not spare my efforts to see that they do."

Pity the orphans under Mr. Bron's tender care, Ben thought. He had forgotten his father's offer to the Five Points Mission in New York City to bring four of its orphans to Bellfield. His pa had written to Uncle Hiram, who volunteered at the mission, to arrange for their transportation on one of the orphan trains to Rockport, Illinois, and from there by steamboat to Bellfield. The Five Points Mission would send its four orphans along with those from the Children's Aid Society of New York. The railroads gave reduced fares to the orphans who traveled on special trains to the Midwest, where they would be placed in homes.

"But what was all that Mr. Blake said about orphans and hard work?" he asked Jamie as they walked home.

Jamie looked serious. "Some of the orphans are indentured. That means the law says they have to work for whoever takes them until they are twenty-one for boys, eighteen for girls. They are supposed to learn a trade like farming or housewifery. In return for work they get food, clothes, and some schooling. Maybe for a man like Luke Henry, a body might work hard till he's twenty-one, but it's risky not knowing what kind of place you might end up in." Jamie's face clouded. "If he means me, I guess I know something about hard work. Guess I still had it better than a lot of orphans. Some get adopted, but some get what they call placed out, just to anyone who wants them, mostly for free labor, and others are indentured. Anyone who takes indentured orphans is supposed to give two suits of clothes and one hundred-fifty dollars to the boys when their time is up, and one hundred dollars and clothes to the girls. It's legal, but I know some orphans end up no different from being the family slave till they are old enough to get away."

Ben nodded. "The same kind of things happen back in New York too. I don't think I could stand it if I was like some of those nine-year-old orphans indentured out till they reach twenty-one. I guess my pa is counting on the good people of Bellfield to take in the orphans when they come." They were at the split in the path where Jamie would go one way and he the other.

"I'll see you tomorrow," Ben said. As he walked toward the cabin he wondered. What if God had let him be an orphan? Would he be living in some workhouse back in New York, or maybe placed out, or like Jamie on a farm working for a man like Jory?

His mother was smiling as he entered the kitchen. "Two letters today, son. This one is for you." She held up a letter that looked official. "Aunt Hett and Uncle Hiram send their love. Our orphans will be arriving in Bellfield next week. Isn't that wonderful?" his mother said. "Just think of those children coming out of the city to all this fresh air and a whole new life."

Ben hoped it would be a good thing. His letter was from Zack. This one, so soon after Zack's last letter, was short and to the point.

"Dear Ben: I am being transferred. By the time you get this I will be somewhere on the way to the Shenandoah Valley in Virginia. My new officer seems like he is okay. I will write you more, soon as I get settled. Yours truly, Zack." "He doesn't say much, just that he is being sent to Virginia," Ben said as he handed the letter to his mother.

"He must have been in a hurry. He doesn't even mention Chaplain Turner."

His mother's face looked serious. "He does say he is under a new commanding officer. I know Chaplain Turner meant to keep Zack with him as an assistant. What could have happened?"

Ben took the letter back and read it again. He felt in his bones that something was wrong. Maybe the chaplain had died of the smallpox. But why hadn't Zack said so? Whatever it was, he would have to wait for Zack's next letter to find out. The fact that Zack was an orphan suddenly struck Ben.

6

Orphans

A crowd of people from the town and surround-ing farms huddled in the light rain that fell. Some were curious onlookers; the rest waited for the steamboat and the orphans due to arrive momentarily. Three of the orphans, two of them boys of thirteen and fourteen, had already been spoken for by local farmers who needed their help. A third, a girl of six, would go to a childless couple. Ben knew the middle-aged man and his frail little wife from church. Even from this distance as he stood by his father, Ben could see the eagerness on the face of the woman. In her hand she gripped a brightly colored woolen shawl ready for her new daughter.

The fourth, a ten-year-old girl, had not yet been chosen as far as Ben knew. Few farmers wanted a girl that age. If she were a boy Ben's father might have taken her in, but with just the loft where Ben slept it wasn't possible.

Glancing around to see who might be willing to take the girl, Ben spotted Miss Ceil and Jamie. A little way off to one side stood Jory. His clothes and boots were caked with dirt, and his eyes had a hard look. As Ben watched, Judge Chatforth handed a paper to Jory, who put his mark on it and thrust it back into the judge's hand. But what was Jory doing here? Then it dawned on Ben. The paper with Jory's mark must be a paper for one of the orphans. Did he mean to take the girl? Shocked, Ben tried to catch Jamie's eye, but just then the steamboat pulled into sight. The first passenger to step down was a boy. His face looked older than the rest of him. He was tall and lean, the right sort for farm work. The farmer who had signed for him seemed satisfied, and the two of them soon left in the farmer's wagon.

The second boy, not so tall as the first, searched the crowd as if looking for someone he knew, and seeing no one stood nervously biting his lip. A farmer watched the boy closely for a few seconds then moved forward to claim him, and with a firm hand on the lad's shoulder led him away.

Meanwhile, the youngest girl was lifted down by Ben's father and carried over to her new family. Ben watched as the couple hugged her tightly. The little one, with her fair skin and thick mop of yellow curls, even looked a bit like them. Wrapped in her new shawl and clasped in the woman's arms the child smiled happily. Ben felt warm inside over the couple's open joy.

Miss Ceil and Jamie stood waiting while the last passenger, the girl Ben thought no one wanted, picked up her small box of belongings. She barely reached Jamie's shoulder and was thin as a rail. Astonished, Ben saw Miss Ceil put an arm about the child's shoulders and lead her away. Jamie followed, carrying the well-worn box.

Jory scowled. "Didn't get her for no coddling," he hollered after them. "Them as don't work, don't eat," he added. Ben heard him mutter, "Blamed fool to bother," as he walked back up to town.

Ben greeted his father with a frown. "Pa, I can't figure why old Jory took on that orphan girl. He ain't fit company for Miss Ceil, even if she is his sister, nor Jamie either."

"The judge and I talked about that, son. The way I see it, Miss Ceil really needs that girl. And for once, Jory's done something decent for his sister. The child will be companionship, and in time she'll learn the things a fine woman like Miss Ceil can teach her. It won't always be easy with a man like Jory, but maybe this is just the kind of thing to soften him up a bit." Ben's father laid his hand lightly on Ben's shoulder. "Don't worry, son, we plan to keep an eye on Jory as well as the others who took in orphans."

As they walked together toward the wagon, Ben thought about Jory's temper and Jamie's accounts of his drunken rampages. He wasn't so sure as the judge or his father that anything could help change Jory. Tomorrow he would find out from Jamie what was going on. Ahead of him he saw Jory head straight to the saloon.

Back at the farm Jamie helped with supper. Miss Ceil fussed over the new girl, piling her plate high with stew and fresh biscuits. Her name was Sissy. Jamie groaned inwardly, knowing already what boys like Thomas Wickens would do with a name like that. He could see himself defending her in the school yard. The girl ate hungrily, as Jamie watched. Maybe she would put on a few needed pounds, so long as their own supplies held steady. And just maybe, he thought, I can teach her to defend herself with a few tricks against the school bullies. They could begin by changing her name.

"How'd it be if we called you Sis?" he asked.

"I think Sissy is a lovely name," put in Miss Ceil, "but they do say that a nickname, a shortened way of saying your name, is a sign of affection. I rather like Sis," she added.

The girl stopped eating. "Sis," she whispered. Then more loudly, "Sis. It's a lot quicker to say. You can call me Sis," she pronounced solemnly.

"Well, Sis, tomorrow is the fair to benefit our soldiers. It ought to be a good place to introduce you to a few folks," Jamie said.

But it was not to be. Sis and Jamie were long gone to bed by the time Jory arrived home. Miss Ceil sat half asleep in a rocking chair by the stove. Startled by the slamming of the back door, she sat up stiffly. "Is that you, Jory?" she asked lightly.

"Course it's me. Who'd you think it'd be this time of night?" His voice was thick, but he could still walk uprightly. He had been drinking, but not yet enough to drown his reason.

"Jory, I'm right glad you got the child. She seems to fit in nicely."

"Better fit," Jory snarled. "Didn't get her for nothing else. Just you see she learns her place around here. Set her to scrubbing first thing tomorrow."

"She'll be a big help to me, truly. But tomorrow's the fair, and since Jamie and I will be going, I'll just take her along. She can help me there."

Jory swung round, his eyes glaring. "That girl ain't going to no fair. The first minute she's here you want to go treating her like she was a guest instead of a worker. She can stay here where she belongs and mind the place."

"But, Jory, she's just a child," Miss Ceil pleaded.

"You stop right there, you hear?" Jory thundered, slamming his fist against the table. "If there was a boat going back to that orphanage, I'd put her on it. Don't know why I did such a blame fool thing anyway, taking on another mouth to feed. She stays home, and that's final." He had said all he would say and stomped out of the kitchen. Miss Ceil covered her face with her hands and wept.

In the morning Jory took his dogs and left before breakfast. There was no telling when he'd be back. He might even go straight to the fair. Miss Ceil busied herself making pancakes. She would let the child sleep a while longer. How could she tell her that there would be no fair for her? Her very first day, and she would be all alone in a strange house. A tear ran down Miss Ceil's cheek, and she brushed it away. There was nothing she could do short of staying home herself, and Jamie was counting so on her going. Luke Henry would be there too. She set her lips in a firm line. For Jamie's sake she would go. And if something came of Luke Henry she would take both Jamie and the child with her away from this miserable place.

The pies were packed, and it was time to leave for the fair. Jamie's face still wore a look of anger as it had all morning. He was all for taking Sis and never minding Jory.

"You know Jory," Miss Ceil said. "He's capable of anything. He just might send Sis back or put her up for hire."

The thought of that was awful even to Jamie. "Okay then," he said, "but how you gonna tell her?" Sis was out fetching spring water, a job she had asked for.

"I'll think of something," Miss Ceil said. "Just let me tell her my way."

At first Sis's eyes had filled with tears, but now she was all attention.

"So you see, dear," Miss Ceil said, "I know you are disappointed, just as I am, but we will both be making a sacrifice for our soldiers. You will be here tending the home front. Someone has to feed the chickens and make sure that they don't get out. And if Mr. Jory comes home you'll have his supper all ready." She pointed to a pot set well back on the stove. "All you have to do is dish out the stew, place the biscuits on the table, and a mug for coffee. There's even coffee keeping warm right here." The coffee pot sat next to the stew pot. "And of course, there is an apple pie. Best of all, I've packed you a surprise dinner right in this pail, and you can eat it outside like a picnic, or inside if you prefer. I do think a picnic is more fun, don't you?"

Sis took the pail eagerly. "Yes, ma'am, and I won't forget the chickens or anything."

"That's a good girl," Miss Ceil said. "And don't wait up for Mr. Jory. If he doesn't come by eight, you just go along upstairs to bed. I'll peek in on you as soon as I come back. We won't be too late, dear." She hugged the child. "Now where has Jamie got to? I need him to help carry these pies."

As if he had heard, Jamie came into the kitchen through the back door. In his hands was a young brown rabbit. "Thought you might like company while we're gone," he said.

"A live rabbit!" Sis squealed with delight. Gently she took it into her hands and touched its little pink nose.

"She'll eat some of that lettuce gone to seed in the garden and a few of the greens. Made you a string collar to put round her neck so's you can tie the other end of the string to the fence while you're busy. Found her inside a hollow tree. The dogs must have gotten the mother. I reckon she'll think you're her mother now."

Sis's face lit with pleasure as she held the soft creature close to her. "I'll name her before you get back," she said.

On the road to the fair, Miss Ceil turned to Jamie. "That was the best gift you could have given Sis."

Jamie's face reddened. "Guess everybody needs something to call their own," he said.

7

The Fair

Tables and booths for the fair filled the clearing just outside of town where a narrow stream ran past a stand of butternut trees. By midday folks were arriving from all over. As Ben searched the crowd for Jamie, Thomas Wickens and his bunch strode by headed toward the stream. Finally, Ben spotted Jamie and Miss Ceil standing near one of the booths.

"Afternoon, Miss Ceil," Ben said. "Those pies sure do look great."

A soft, pleased look lit Miss Ceil's face. "Well, thanks to Jamie's apples and sugar, they do seem to have turned out well. I hope they will sell."

"You selling any by the slice?" Ben asked. "'Cause right now I'm ready for a piece."

"What a good idea, Ben," Miss Ceil said. "If you'll come back in an hour I'll see what I can do." Her soft blue eyes were merry. "You go along with Ben, Jamie. I'll be fine here."

As they walked, Ben questioned Jamie about the orphan girl Jory had signed for. Jamie's voice sounded angry. "I reckon he took her because he's too tightfisted to hire any help."

"My pa thinks it might be a good thing for Miss Ceil to have the girl with her," Ben said. "But with old Jory around, I wonder what will come of it. By the way, where is the girl?"

"Jory wouldn't let her come. It makes me want to shake the meanness out of him," Jamie said. "The sooner Miss Ceil leaves and takes Sis with her, the better. That reminds me, I'm needing to make sure Luke Henry knows Miss Ceil's here."

"You think Luke Henry's wanting to court Miss Ceil?" Ben asked.

"Well, maybe he needs a little shove, but I know he looks like spring's here every time he sees Miss Ceil," Jamie answered.

"But supposing Luke Henry won't take on Sis, or maybe Jory won't let her go. He's the one who signed for her, and that makes him legally in charge of her, right?" Ben said.

Jamie stared at Ben. "Luke Henry don't worry me none, but all that about Jory having the say over who gets Sis, that might be a parcel of trouble. I've gotta think on it. Jory better not stand in the way." A look of determination set his mouth in a grim line.

The two made their way toward a part of the field where games were already in progress. "Isn't that Luke Henry over there?" Ben asked, pointing at a tall dark-haired man waiting his turn in the iron horseshoe pitch. Though the young man limped, favoring his right leg, his shoulders were broad and his arms muscular. As the boys watched he pitched first one, then each of the others directly onto the pole.

Jamie let out a low whistle. "That's Luke. I hear he's a crack shot too." A sad note entered his voice. "Guess he might still be fighting with our northern boys against the southern rebs if he hadn't nearly lost his leg in the fighting." Ben had seen a lot of the North's Union soldiers who had come back wounded from this war, and he knew many more would never come back.

Jamie led the way over to Luke Henry and greeted him. "Hear tell, Miss Ceil's selling some mighty good apple pies over yonder next to the Dolans' table." He grinned up at Luke.

"You don't say, Jamie," Luke said as he laid one large hand on Jamie's shoulder. "You think I'd best be getting over there before she sells out?"

"Reckon I sure wouldn't let no grass grow under my feet if they was in your shoes," Jamie said. Mischief danced in Jamie's eyes, and he winked at Ben.

Going along with Jamie, Ben said in a worried voice, "Maybe we ought to go buy some for ourselves before they're gone."

"Good idea, but since we're here, may as well try out a few things," Jamie said.

Luke Henry looked thoughtful. "Why don't you boys just take my place for a while?" he suggested. "I'm feeling mighty hungry." He patted Jamie's head and took off toward the booths.

Ben grinned. "Bet his hunger won't be satisfied

with anything less than Miss Ceil's apple pie." Jamie smiled back as he picked up an iron horseshoe.

By supper time Miss Ceil's pies were all sold. Luke had bought the last two. Miss Ceil blushed as she tucked away the money Luke handed her. "You already bought one earlier. Are you sure you want two more?" she said.

Luke put both pies off to one side of the table. "What I want is to take you to supper, Miss Ceil, and I don't plan on waiting another minute. That is, if you're agreeable?"

"Oh, Luke Henry, you are impossible." She couldn't help smiling at him. "The truth is, I would love some supper." She let him take her arm and lead her to the booths where delicious smells of hot food and spiced cider wafted over the customers.

They ate under an oak tree where Luke had spread a flour sack to sit on. For a long time Luke listened as Miss Ceil talked. Now and then he asked a question.

Far enough away so they couldn't hear but could still see Luke Henry and Miss Ceil, Ben and Jamie sat munching hot meat pies. Jamie glanced at the couple. "Looks like they're enjoying themselves," he said triumphantly as if he alone had mastered the whole thing.

Some folks had already left, but others gathered around a small band of musicians, most of them brothers from a German immigrant family. A huge bonfire cast its warmth and light, and lanterns glowed from poles around the space cleared for dancing. In minutes laughter, clapping, and the stomping of feet filled the brisk evening air as several couples joined in a folk dance. Hilda Loos, whose father played the violin, took hold of her friend Tessie Blake's hands, and the two of them twirled to the lively music. Ben noticed that his father was clapping his large hands loudly to the rhythm. His mother looked as if she would gladly have danced if anyone asked her. Suddenly, Ben's father swooped her into his arms and danced her onto the field.

Not far from where Ben stood, Mrs. Kent, one of the ladies of the church, looked horrified. "Why, I never!" she exclaimed. "A minister of the gospel has no business dancing. He'd never have gotten our vote if we'd known that. Come, Joshua," she called turning away from the scene. "It's time decent folks went home."

"Now, Elizabeth, it ain't all that bad. Some Christian folks don't hold to dancing, others do. I can't rightly believe folk dancing does a body harm," Joshua said as he followed his wife dutifully.

Ben was about to comment, when Jamie burst out, "There's Luke and Miss Ceil!" The two, who had stood close to the ring of dancers, were now dancing together.

Jamie's plan seemed to be working. "Jamie, you thinking of staying round if Miss Ceil and Luke Henry marry?" Ben asked.

"Haven't got that far yet. One thing's for sure, you won't find me hanging round Jory's place," Jamie said.

"Reckon not," Ben agreed. "Course, there's still Bron and his cane. Suppose you won't want to stick around for that anymore."

Jamie didn't answer for minute. "Don't rightly know," he confessed.

Ben said no more. What would it be like for him if Jamie left? Would he be able to stand it by himself? Except for Will Coster, Ben hadn't made friends with Wickens and his bunch. Ben was still an outsider. Anyway, he'd had his fill of bullies like Wickens back east.

A bright moon hung above them by the time the last wagon loaded up. Luke Henry had offered Miss Ceil and Jamie a ride home, and Ben climbed into the wagon behind his father. The sound of a galloping horse made them all look up. A man riding hard tore into the clearing.

He pulled his horse to a stop and shouted, "Miss Ceil, there's a fire over to your place! It looks bad. You better come quick!"

All over the clearing men's voices broke out in hurried commands. Ben saw Miss Ceil's white face turn to Luke Henry. "The child, Luke. Oh, hurry, please hurry!" she cried. Luke forced the horses into a run.

Ben's father called out, "We're coming with you," and turned the wagon to follow Luke's. "Hang on," he warned. Ben clung to the wagon seat as the horse raced and the wagon wheels bumped along. In the distance a red glare against the sky came into sight.

8

Fire!

Ben could see the red flames leaping as they came closer. His father brought the wagon to a stop, threw the reins to Ben's mother, and ran toward the burning house. Ben ran after him. His mother's voice called behind him, "You be careful, Ben."

Ben lifted a hand to show that he heard, but he didn't stop running. Several men were already forming a bucket line, and others brought buckets of water from the well to them. The fire seemed to engulf the half of the house it had not already destroyed.

Jamie stood staring at the flames. His face was deathly white, and his eyes never left the scene in front of them as Ben came to stand by him.

A flash of memory sent chills down Ben's neck. Jamie's folks had died in a fire only two years before, during the Indian uprising. Ben searched for something to say and then thought of the orphan girl, Sis. Was she trapped somewhere inside the house? If you could call it a house. The roof had burst into flames with a loud noise as great chunks of it fell. The men with their small buckets backed away. Nothing could save the farmhouse now.

Ben's mother came by with Miss Ceil who looked

about to faint. Two women Ben didn't know and Tessie Blake's mother came to help.

Mrs. Blake put her arm around Miss Ceil's shoulder and, with a voice half choked in tears, offered her lodging till she could get back on her feet.

Deathly pale, Miss Ceil tried to thank her, but instead a cry of anguish wrenched from her lips. "The child! I should never have left her." It was all she could manage before great sobs convulsed her.

Ben felt Jamie stir beside him. "Maybe she got out somehow," he said.

"We need to look for her!" Jamie cried. He hesitated for a moment, then started in the direction of the house.

"Wait, Jamie," Ben called. Nobody could go into that inferno.

The heat of the flames stopped Jamie, and Ben caught up with him. "She's got to be somewhere," Jamie shouted. "Maybe she hid out back." As he turned and ran, Ben rushed after him. The roof of the outhouse had been soaked to keep it from catching fire. Pulling open the door, Jamie cried, "Sis," but it was empty. "The barn! She has to be there."

The barn stood away from the house, and the fire had not yet reached it. All of the animals had already been led out to safety. There was no sign of Sis. Jamie looked as if he couldn't believe that the girl wasn't here. Running from stall to stall he searched. Behind him, Ben said softly, "She's not here or they would have found her, wouldn't they?"

"She's got to be somewhere. I know she's hid-ing," Jamie insisted. "Too scared to come out. The cornfield! How could I forget the cornfield?" He turned to go when something brown and white moved under the hay near Jamie's foot. "The rabbit!" Jamie cried.

Quickly he scooped up hay by the handfuls. Ben helped, and together they made an opening in the huge mound. Burrowed under the hay, curled up in a frightened little ball, lay Sis.

"Sis, you okay?" Jamie asked. He lifted her up. Tears streamed down her face.

"I didn't do it," she whispered. "I did just what Miss Ceil told me. Only Jory came home, and he yelled at me." Her voice quivered, and her small body shook. "He said I didn't know how to build a fire, and he'd teach me. He kept piling on wood, and piling it on." Her voice quivered, and her body shook. "He just kept drinking whiskey and piling on wood. When the wood box was empty he started breaking up the kitchen chairs and throwing them on too. Sparks were flying everywhere, and I begged him to stop, but he wouldn't. He wanted the rabbit, but I wouldn't let him have it. I ran out and hid in here." She began to cry hard.

Jamie patted her head. "It wasn't your fault. You did the right thing to run out. Come on, now. Miss Ceil's half dead with worry for you."

Ben followed as Jamie led the girl out of the barn. As the men and women battling the fire saw them come the crowd cheered mightily. Jamie went straight to the wagon where Miss Ceil was sitting up, a dazed look on her face.

"Sis!" she cried holding out her arms to the girl, who ran directly to them. Between tears and thanksgiving Miss Ceil held Sis tightly and listened to her story. Sorrow for her brother gripped her. Jory was dead. From the grim remains, Luke Henry thought, Jory must have fallen and been trapped in the burning house. But the joy of the child's return seemed to give Miss Ceil strength.

A swift shadow of pain passed over her face as she looked up at Jamie who stood silently watching the two. Without a word she opened her arms to him and drew him close in the little circle that held Sis.

Ben felt a lump in his own throat. He started as a hand closed on his shoulder. His father's face, streaked with soot, looked down at him. "We wondered, your mother and I, if Jamie might like to stay with you for a while."

"He can sleep in the loft with me," Ben offered.

His father addressed Miss Ceil. "My dear, if you are willing, Jamie can stay with us for as long as he likes. You and the child are welcome at the Blakes."

Miss Ceil lifted her head. "God bless you. It would be a kindness to us until we're able to be together."

Ben's father reached out and took Jamie's hand in his own. "And you, son, are you willing to give us a try?"

"Thank you, sir. I'd be right glad of that," Jamie replied.

"Come along, then. There's no need of my presence here any more tonight," Ben's father said.

Sunday dawned cold and gray. The folks gathered for Jory's funeral listened quietly by the graveside as Ben's father spoke. Ben stood by Jamie. Miss Ceil held tightly to Sis's hand and wept gently for her brother. Ben knew most folks had come for Miss Ceil's sake rather than Jory's.

The following week Ben and Jamie walked to school. Ben's mother had made a good school outfit for Jamie, and his father had bought him a solid pair of leather boots similar to Ben's. Ben smiled to himself. The two of them might be brothers, except of course for Jamie's red hair.

Ben slipped into his seat next to Thomas Wickens. Sis was already seated in her place with the younger girls. Her brown hair looked neat under a dark blue bow that matched her dress. Though she sat like a frozen statue, Ben saw the faintest flicker of a smile brush her mouth as Jamie turned to glance her way.

From the front of the room the sharp voice of Mr. Bron cut through the air. "Master Hill, you will turn this way, sir." The cane in Mr. Bron's hand tapped warningly against the desk top. "I will expect behavior toward your betters in keeping with what your benefactors have done to make you respectable. Now let us get on with the day." The two new orphan boys seated near Jamie looked wide-eyed at their new schoolmaster.

"Jamie Hill's still a nobody," Thomas whispered next to Ben "He bloody-well better not put on airs."

"Some people don't have to put on airs," Ben said glaring at Thomas. He wanted to say more, but he held it in. Why should he risk Bron's cane? The Wickenses came to church, and Ben knew that both Mr. Wickens and his wife had strong opinions. Mr. Wickens had lots to say, and he always seemed to start by saying "Now the way I see you ought to handle this is . . . "

At lunchtime, Sis ran across the yard to where Ben and Jamie sat. "I can't stay," she said breathing hard. "Tessie says now that I'm living with them I've got to keep with her and the other girls." She lowered her voice. "But don't you worry none, Jamie. Miss Ceil said to tell you soon's she can we'll all be together like before. Oh, I almost forgot, she said to tell you Mr. Dolan is letting her work afternoons helping out at his store for a while."

Jamie nodded. "Thanks. If you need me, you know where to find me, Sis." He smiled up at her.

"I won't ever forget you, Jamie," Sis said solemnly. Someone called her name, and Sis turned to look. "Tessie wants me. I have to go now," she said. "Don't forget us," she called over her shoulder as she hurried off.

Ben grinned at Jamie. "She'd be a hard one to forget," he said. "Seems like Tessie Blake's looking out for her okay."

Jamie's eyes had a faraway look. "There's ways of looking out and there's other ways. Could be

Tessie likes having somebody to fetch for her. I don't know."

"There's worse jobs," Ben said. "Most of the orphans at the Five Points Mission where Sis was came off the streets half starved and wandering around without a roof over their heads."

Jamie looked at Ben. "Maybe so, but Sis is no servant, and besides that, Miss Ceil plans to adopt her as soon as she can."

"Hold on," Ben said quickly. "I was just meaning Sis looks like she can handle Tessie Blake okay. Like you said, it's only for a while. Besides, I reckon Tessie wants Sis to join up with the rest of the girls against the boys—me in particular."

The warning bell clanged loudly, and Ben heaved a sigh. A curious thought crossed his mind. Where had Sis come from before she lived in the Five Points Mission? Maybe she didn't even know who her folks had been.

Across the yard Tessie Blake marched, with Sis right behind her carrying two lunch pails. Hilda, on Sis's left, carried the hoops the girls had used in a game.

Quick as a hawk Jamie grabbed Ben's lunch pail. Before Ben could figure out what was happening, Jamie strode ahead of him whistling and swinging both lunch pails. With a shout, Ben ran after him. Through clenched teeth Jamie whispered, "I'll explain later." Puzzled, Ben let him keep both pails.

At the end of the day, Sis had already gone with

Tessie and the girls when Jamie picked up his own lunch pail. He made no move to pick up Ben's.

Ben took up his own pail none too gently. "So what was that all about with the pails this noon?" he asked.

"Sorry if you're feeling put out, Ben," Jamie said. "Just thought it might make Sis feel better, you know." His face reddened.

For a minute Ben didn't speak. "You wanted her to think you had to fetch and carry for me, same as she's doing for Tessie?" Ben asked quietly.

"Sort of dumb, I guess," Jamie replied. "Sometimes I don't make sense even to myself. No hard feelings, eh, Ben?" Jamie stood still. "I know you and me ain't like that. I reckon with Miss Ceil and Sis and me it was sort of instant kin. I know Mrs. Blake is a charitable woman, but it's different. To the Blakes Sis is no more than a hired girl."

Ben searched Jamie's face. "Never thought about all that," he said slowly. "I reckon as soon as Miss Ceil and Luke Henry get married Sis won't have to worry none about fetching for Tessie Blake." He stopped and grinned at Jamie. "Just so you know your place, last one home does all the chores."

Jamie smiled. "You're on, friend."

As they raced, Ben's lunch pail banged against his side. If Jamie wanted to pretend for Sis's sake by carrying his lunch pail, why should he mind? Ahead of him Jamie ran like the wind. Ben doubled his efforts to catch up with him. Jamie wasn't pretending now.

9

Trouble

Ben sat rigidly in the front pew of the church. He had known there would be trouble over the Indians when his father called for this meeting. Angry murmurs rose all around them. The speaker, Mr. Hinman, a missionary to the Indians, was seated next to his father behind the pulpit. He was a thin, plainly dressed man with a kind face that looked calmly at the crowd. Jamie, sitting next to Ben whispered, "It sounds to me like some folks ain't too pleased to see Mr. Hinman."

At first the crowd quieted as Mr. Hinman began to talk. "As you good folk in Bellfield know," he said, "not all the Sioux Indians took part in the uprising. Some of you may even be here today because of the brave actions of those Indians who risked their lives to save white settlers. For their heroism they became outcasts from the rest of their tribe. But instead of receiving our thanks, they, too, were not allowed to return to their homes on the old reservation." He paused and looked around. "In fact, ladies and gentlemen, at this very moment families of these Indians who proved themselves our friends are in desperate need. They are homeless, hungry, cold, many of them sick. As you well know, they are in danger of being killed if they set foot outside the camp Brother Faribault provides them on part of his farm." His voice grew loud as he said, "The bounty the army pays for Indian scalps does not recognize the difference between friend or foe so long as that scalp belongs to an Indian!" Ben shuddered as he listened. "Our government forbids them freedom in Minnesota, yet the law passed over a year ago made promises to those Indians who risked their lives for white settlers. I believe the time has come to keep those promises. Only yesterday I received word that the government is willing to look into the matter. Ladies and gentlemen, we must bring our red brothers back to live in peace!"

As Mr. Hinman explained that the government was ready to give each of the friendly Indians eighty acres of land back on their old reservation, the mood of the crowd changed.

Deacon Blake stood to his feet commanding attention. "My friends," he said, "I hold no personal grudge in my heart against these Indians, outcasts of their own people. But can we afford to allow them or any Indians to go back to their old reservation? Hostile Indians still make their way through our guards. Only recently a white family was murdered on their way to a new settlement in Wright County. I say the risk is too great."

"But, sir," Mr. Hinman objected, "the isolated killing you speak of was done by hostile, not Christian, Indians." His voice was drowned out by the protests of others.

"General Sibley says Minnesota frontiers won't be safe till the army rounds up every last hostile Sioux," someone called out. "And from the looks of it, the general says, there are more of them banding together out in Dakota and clear up to Canada."

"They was all friendly Indians one time. Who's to say when an Indian will turn back to his savage ways?" cried another man.

Ben saw the elderly widow of Will's uncle stand to her feet, pale and shaking. A hush came over the crowd. With a quivering voice the woman made her plea. "Deacon Blake is right. You all know that my dear husband was murdered in the Indian raids at New Ulm. You must not allow the Indians to go back to their old ways. Never again. They must learn to live like white folks, but not in Minnesota!"

Deacon Blake moved to stand beside the old lady. "What we must do is sign a petition to the governor protesting any return of Indians to their old reservation. No land grants will be tolerated! I propose to see to it that the governor hears of this if I have to go to St. Paul myself!"

"No Indians!" Mr. Wickens shouted. "I'll sign that petition. We won't let them come back."

Several men and women took up the cry, "No Indians." A few voices begged them to think of the innocent, the friendly Indians, but it was useless.

Ben's father brought the meeting to a close. He spoke quietly of the need for healing and mercy, then dismissed the people with a prayer. He prayed first for the United States torn apart by civil war between brothers in the north and brothers in the south, and then for Minnesota still suffering from the war between her white brothers and her red brothers. Ben heard Mr. Wickens mutter, "Ain't no southerner and no red man brothers of mine."

Tears flowed down Ben's mother's face. Brokenly she whispered, "That is the end of all Mr. Hinman's work. The Indians will never be allowed to go back to their homes now." On the platform Mr. Hinman sat with his head bowed. A few people, Miss Ceil among them, went to offer him their sympathy.

As folks left, Ben saw Deacon Blake corner his father. That meant trouble.

While they waited for his pa, Ben and Jamie walked around to the back of the church to the little cemetery. "Reckon Deacon Blake's laying it on your pa again," Jamie said brushing the dirt from a small gravestone. "He'd choke before he'd pray for Indians."

"My pa's got a way of finding trouble. It's not the first time. We left Tarrytown, New York, because of it."

Jamie looked hard at Ben. "You mean he preached against the war?"

Ben replied defiantly, "He supports the Union's cause, but Pa insists on praying for folks on both sides." He went on in a softer voice, "It's things like that, and speaking out for fairness no matter

what a person's color is, that get him in trouble."
Ben frowned. "It's hard to explain."

"Sort of like praying for Indians," Jamie said quietly. "Miss Ceil used to pray for the Indians every night. She says forgiving someone who does a terrible thing isn't natural. But it's easier when we think how God forgives us for what we do, and if he didn't, none of us could ever get into heaven. An Indian named Joseph saved my life. He and his friend John Other Day helped me and other white settlers escape in the uprising."

Ben bit his lip. He had almost forgotten that Jamie's folks had been killed in the Indian uprising two years before. "Guess you're right," he said. "But there's folks who don't see things that way." Just then Ben's mother called.

As the boys neared the wagon they slowed to a standstill. Mr. Bron and another man stood by the wagon. The gentleman beside him, though shorter and heavier built, had a strong resemblance to the schoolmaster with his long chin and high brow.

"My cousin, Mr. Jasper Rockforth from St. Paul," Mr. Bron said, bowing slightly. Deacon Blake and Ben's father came to join the group as Ben and Jamie quietly slipped around to the back of the wagon.

On the way home Ben's mother remarked, "At least one good thing came out of this dreadful meeting. It seems Mr. Bron's cousin is going south to teach former slaves. Many of them have escaped to the Union forces. And now that our army holds so much of the South, the freed slaves are homeless.

Most of them can't read or write. His work will be much appreciated."

"Yes," Ben's father agreed. "He can use all the books, blankets, and clothes we can spare. I hear things are in short supply in the camps the government has set up for the freed slaves. Maybe this town can do something to help former slaves even if they refuse to help their former Indian friends." Ben knew he meant the friendly Indians who had helped white settlers.

In Mr. Bron's room Jasper Rockforth faced his cousin. "Why don't you throw in your luck with me? There's plenty of money to be made off the goodhearted folks in the north, and we don't have to do a thing but spend it. Sooner or later someone is going to find out how you served time in jail for mishandling that orphan's fund, and then where will you be?"

Mr. Bron's face grew dark. "I hardly think anyone here in this forsaken prairie town will learn of my past unless you intend to tell them, cousin." He cast a stern look at Mr. Rockforth. "No, I suppose not you, since you have your own secrets. If it had not been for that meddling minister and those sniveling orphans he managed to get to, I would still be headmaster at the Philadelphia orphanage and living in comfort. A curse on all orphans and ministers!" A deep scowl twisted his face as he paced back and forth in the room. "What you propose has its risks. However, together we might make something profitable from it. I will give what you say some thought, cousin."

By Wednesday the ladies of the Christian Aid Society had organized a drive to contribute to the work of Mr. Rockforth. At school, whoever could brought pennies to place in an envelope in Mr. Bron's desk drawer. Some, like Tessie Blake, brought larger sums of money. Mr. Bron himself urged the class to work hard for the needy, former slaves. Several times he spoke of Mr. Rockforth's work and reminded the class to spread the word at home.

After school Ben remarked, "Can't figure the change in Mr. Bron. He is the last one I would guess to care about helping the freed slaves."

"Maybe that cousin of his made him see the light," Jamie said. "You notice, Bron hasn't used his cane all week? You reckon we could put up a petition for his cousin to stay around here till spring? Or better still, take Bron with him when he goes?"

Both boys ended up laughing helplessly as Jamie mimicked Jasper Rockforth's overly polite manners, and Ben pretended an equally polite Mr. Bron's responses between slaps of a stick cane against his leg.

As they barged into the kitchen, Ben's mother, with tears in her eyes, looked at them solemnly. Ben rushed to her side, and she clasped him to her. "What's happened?" he asked. His throat felt tight with fear.

10

The Death of a Friend

O h, Ben," she said, "I'm so sorry. There's been a terrible incident. Chaplain Turner himself wrote the letter as soon as he learned what happened." With a trembling hand she placed the paper stamped with the Union eagle in Ben's hand. "Our dear Zack is dead, son."

Ben stared at his mother. "Zack?" Without waiting for an answer he looked at the letter in his hand. "It is my sad duty to inform you of the death of Zack . . ." Ben stopped reading. A lump filled his throat. He pushed past Jamie out the kitchen door and ran blindly to the barn.

No one followed him. In the dim coolness of the barn Ben read the rest of the letter. "In a surprise attack on the supply wagons Zack was captured. The attackers, the infamous Mosby's raiders, fled deep into the Blue Ridge Mountains. Our men rode after them catching up with the stragglers, and during the fighting Zack was shot and thrown from his captor's horse. There was no time to retrieve his body then or later as the chase continued into the night far into mountainous territory known to the raiders but unfamiliar to our men." For a long time

Ben sat still. His legs cramped under him at last, and the pain forced him to move.

Had Zack died from the gunshot or been left alone to die in the mountains? An ant crawled over the back of Ben's hand. He lifted it up close and let it climb part way up his arm. A small scar shaped like an X still showed white on his forearm where he had cut it the day a drunken soldier had cut an X on Zack's back. It was the sign that they were blood brothers. It didn't matter that Zack was black and he was white; nothing could separate them, until now.

"Why couldn't you just come home?" Tears of anger flowed down Ben's face. It felt like some deep part of him had suddenly been cut out. Nothing would ever be the same again. From the day Zack had gone off to war, things had changed. Now Zack wasn't coming back ever.

How long he sat rocking back and forth in his grief Ben didn't know. The barn grew dark. Still he didn't move. When the door opened and footsteps approached, he didn't look up.

"May I sit down?" his father asked and sat down, though Ben did not answer. "I loved him too. We all did," his father said. Then strong arms were around him holding him close. Ben felt his father's face wet with tears as he pressed Ben's to him.

After a while his father spoke. "Zack is safe now. And if you can imagine it, son, he is happier than anyone on earth could ever be. You remember when Letti's brother died and he asked us to stay by him till the angels came for him?" Ben nodded. "Zack's angel came for him too, son."

Later when Ben crept up the ladder to the loft, Jamie was already asleep on his pallet. Quietly Ben undressed and lay down. He pulled the blanket above his head.

Early the next morning before anyone was up and about, Ben slipped out to a clearing in a corner of the cornfield. For twenty minutes he dug and shaped the ground until there was a small mound. On its center he set a simple wooden cross he had nailed together the night before. Across it were scratched the words: *Gone Home* and under that *Zack died 1864.*

For a minute he bowed his head, then looked up and said, "Leastwise he's home with you, Lord." He walked away without looking back.

Back in the cabin the smell of frying bacon greeted him. "Pancakes, too," his mother said. "So let's see how many you two can eat and still not be late for school."

There was no time for conversation. The sight of bacon and hot cakes with thick syrup reminded Ben he hadn't had any dinner the night before.

The walk to school seemed longer than usual. They were halfway there when Jamie said, "Ben, for what it's worth, I'm sorry about your friend Zack. Your ma told me about him. Losing a friend like that sure leaves a terrible empty place."

Deep inside Ben the fresh wound threatened to

open. "It's okay," he said. "I just don't want to talk about it."

"Right," Jamie said. "When my folks were killed, it took a long time for me too."

Misery for Jamie flooded Ben and made him swallow hard. "Sorry about your folks," he said. "I guess a body doesn't ever forget a thing like that."

"Reckon not," Jamie replied.

The last students were going in as they arrived at the school, and they hurried to catch up. At the front of the room the schoolmaster stood with the end of his cane poking through the upturned contents of his desk drawer. A hush came over the room as every eye focused on the scene in front of them.

"It is my duty to inform you that among us sits a thief of the lowest order." Mr. Bron's voice was stern and cold and his look fierce as he searched the faces before him.

11

To Catch a Thief

Benjamin Able, come here," Mr. Bron commanded as he tapped his cane impatiently against his desk. No one moved, and it seemed as if the whole class was holding its breath.

With a sinking feeling inside, Ben rose and walked to the front next to the teacher's desk.

"Miss Blake, be so kind as to come and stand by our young friend," Mr. Bron said not taking his eyes from Ben's.

When Tessie approached the desk she stood next to Ben, a puzzled look on her face.

"Now, Miss Blake, you are the class secretary for the charity fund. Please tell us the exact amount at your last count yesterday."

In a small voice Tessie said, "It was four dollars and twenty-five cents, sir."

"Yes, Miss Blake, and did you not write down the amount on this sheet of paper?" Mr. Bron held out a ledger sheet.

"Yes, sir, I did," Tessie replied. "Right there it is, sir." Her finger pointed to a figure on the paper.

"Very well, thank you. You then closed the envelope and returned it to its proper place in the drawer? This duty you carried out at precisely the last ten minutes before class dismissal for the day?"

"Oh, yes, sir. You yourself closed the drawer afterward." Tessie's face was pale as she stared at Ben.

"You may sit down, Miss Blake, thank you." Mr. Bron waited until she returned to her desk before turning to Ben. "And you, sir, did I not ask you to remain at your desk after school until such time as you completed copying an assignment whose details I shall not go into?"

Ben's eyes widened and his face grew warm. "Yes, but I never touched that envelope."

"Indeed," Mr. Bron admonished. "Were you not here alone for a full five minutes while I dismissed the class? And did I not put on my coat and close the door behind me as always to conserve heat in the schoolroom? And were you not alone in this room at that time? Answer the question, sir."

Ben stared at the man before him. This couldn't be happening. Wildly he looked at the desk as if by some strange feat the money might appear. "Yes, sir, I finished the work and laid it on your desk, just as you returned." Ben looked up triumphantly. "There, sir, you came back at that very moment. I couldn't have taken the money." Deliberately Mr. Bron brought his cane to tap lightly on Ben's shoulder. "Oh, but you could, Master Able. Perhaps you finished quickly. A moment to open the drawer, snatch, and who is the wiser? An innocent boy stands at the desk to hand in his work. But innocent, I think not." At his last words a gasp came from somewhere in the room.

Ben's throat tightened as anger and shame burned within him. "I never touched that money," he managed to blurt out.

Mr. Bron glared at Ben, then turned to the class. "Let me refresh your mind. I alone hold the key to this school. It has not left my presence since I last used it yesterday to lock this room upon leaving for the day. The door was still locked this morning when I arrived. Only, our thief had already done his work well before that." With a look of satisfaction he opened his desk drawer. "You may see for yourself, sir, the envelope is gone." As if to prove his point he held the empty draw upside down. Its contents strewn on the desk top were plain to see: the ledger sheet, a ruler, a few small personal items, and a thick sheathe of papers in a loose brown wrapper.

"Well, Master Able, you see where we have come. I am left with no option but to hold you responsible. I shall inform your parents. Though I count this deed contemptible, I shall expect full restitution and an apology. For the present you will remove yourself to the north corner of the room with your face to the wall for the remainder of the day."

Ben's feet refused to move. He felt himself trembling as the horror of what was happening came swirling over him.

"I shall not repeat myself, Master Able. You are to go to the wall at once."

Ben heard the words but stood rooted to the spot. The first stinging swish of the cane surprised him. Instinctively he raised his hands to ward off the next and felt the sharp edge of the slender wood cut across the back of his right hand. Blow followed blow, and though he cowered he did not move.

"Stop!" The ringing shout brought an immediate stop to the beating. Ben hurt so much at first he barely grasped that someone else had come forward. Through watery eyes he saw that the someone was Jamie.

"I'm the one that stole the money," Jamie said deliberately standing tall and defiantly before Mr. Bron.

With a quick motion of the cane Mr. Bron lifted Jamie's chin. "And when did you enter the school to do your deed? Or do I detect a fool's desire here to play the hero for your newfound benefactors?"

Stubbornly Jamie shook his head. "I climbed in the window after dark and left the same way."

Mr. Bron dropped his cane from Jamie's chin. "And what, may I ask, moved you, sir, to come forward? I will have the whole truth." He leaned over Jamie with menace in his eyes. "Perhaps, sir, you and your benefactor's whelp are in cahoots. Did you plan to spend the money together?"

Jamie's face went white, but his eyes flashed with anger. "I did it, and that's all you'll get from me." Murmurs of shock went through the class.

Mr. Bron studied the defiant figure before him. "We shall see, we shall see," he said. "I will deal with you later, sir. Go back to your seat and do not leave it until I say." A strange look came over Mr. Bron's face while he stared at the back of Jamie's retreating form.

Without looking at Ben, he flung the cane to a corner of the desk. "Enough of this interruption to our day. Take yourself out of my sight. The cloakroom will do for you."

Holding his arms stiffly to his sides, Ben made his way blindly past the rows of desks to the small anteroom that served as a cloakroom. Relief flooded over him. At least here no one could see him. He leaned against the cold wall holding his injured arms to his chest. Hanging by itself from a wooden peg above him an old forgotten muffler dangled its ends toward him. He reached for it and buried his burning face in its rough wool. Why hadn't Jamie come forward in the beginning? "Coward," he muttered bitterly. "He let me take his whipping, and all the time he knew he'd done it." Anger choked him. "Coward, coward," he repeated over and over. Not only had Jamie stolen the money, but now Bron thought he was in on it too just because Jamie was staying at his house. It wasn't fair. How could Jamie have done such a lowdown trick as steal money meant for charity?

No one came to the cloakroom, and as the morning wore on the cold crept inside Ben numbing his feet and hands. The heat of the small school stove did not reach this far. On cold windy days it barely warmed those unlucky enough to sit any distance from it.

Ben's thoughts whirled. He shivered and wondered about putting on his coat. If he did, and Bron saw it he might punish him for that too. The muffler was too small to do much good, but he huddled as close to it as he could. Anyway, he'd rather freeze in here than stand in front of the whole school.

At noon the others came to get their lunch buckets, all except Jamie. No one spoke to Ben. Only Sis waved her small hand quickly before she left. From where he stood Ben could see his and Jamie's lunch pails, the only two left. Ben swallowed hard. It served Jamie right.

The noon recess passed, and then midafternoon. For a while he strained to hear the voices from the other room, and then suddenly it was dismissal time. He must have fallen asleep on his feet! Once more there was a scramble for coats and buckets. This time two or three braved a muttered "good luck" as they passed Ben. After what seemed a long time Jamie came in. Mr. Bron was behind him.

"Well, Master Able, has your time alone given you a more willing spirit?" He paused for a second before handing Ben an envelope. "I hardly expected any change from you, sir. You will take this letter to your parents. You will bring an apology upon your return to school. When I have heard the whole truth, I will decide on a suitable punishment." He held Jamie's chin tightly for a few seconds, then without waiting for an answer he left the cloakroom.

At the side of the building Thomas Wickens and his friend Lucas Teachman waited. Thomas looked surprised. "Thought you two were goners for sure," he offered in a friendly manner. Jamie scowled, and Ben did not answer. The two boys fell in step with them anyway. They had walked in silence for about five minutes when Thomas let out, "Hey, where's my pail?" Ben and Jamie kept on walking.

Behind them, Lucas said, "You must'a left it back at school."

"Wait for me, you fellows," Thomas cried.

Ben gave no sign he had heard. Beside him Jamie quickened his pace. By the time they turned off onto a shortcut through the woods Lucas and Thomas were completely out of sight. Angrily Ben continued to walk fast.

"Are you okay, Ben? Hey, slow down."

Ben whirled around to face Jamie. "You knew I had nothing to do with your stealing that money."

Jamie started to say, "Wait a minute, what are you talking about?"

Ben turned angrily away from him. "I don't want to hear it. Just go away and leave me be." He ran ahead leaving a stunned Jamie behind.

Jamie shook his head. Without thinking he walked into the woods as he had done so many times in the days when he still lived with Jory and Miss Ceil. His feet felt heavy, and his shoulders slumped. Maybe nothing would ever change for him. He hadn't taken the money, and he was sure Ben hadn't. But if Ben thought he was the thief, everyone else would too. Glancing around he saw he had been following an old half-hidden path, one he used to take when he needed to be alone. A fallen log lay to one side of the path. He sat on it and let the stillness of the woods seep into him.

All day gray clouds had piled up threatening a storm, and now the first flakes of snow began to fall. A crow nearby began to scold him, and Jamie flicked a pebble toward it, his thoughts racing. The sight of the cane flashing down on Ben's hands and arms had acted like an alarm bell to him. He could not stop himself from getting up and going up to do something, anything to put an end to it. Jamie put his head into his hands. He had said the first thing that popped into his mind, and now what?

For a long time he sat. When he finally got up he knew he could never go back. Miss Ceil would have Luke Henry to look after her. The wedding was set to take place in a week. He wished he could explain at least to Luke Henry and Ben's father. But why should they believe him? It was no use. He had messed up everything. They would be better off without him. Leaving the lunch pail on the ground by the log, he began to walk once more. This time he headed away from Bellfield. Behind him the softly falling snow covered his footprints from sight.

12

A Double Departure

Meanwhile an anxious Thomas raced toward the school. He might not have worried so much over an empty lunch bucket, but it wasn't exactly empty. At noon recess he had won a big blue and two good shooters off Sam Banks. The marbles were inside the pail. The school door stood ajar, and without thinking Thomas rushed in. With a jolt he thudded into Mr. Bron, who was just on his way out. Several books and a thick sheaf of papers in a loose brown wrapper flew from the schoolmaster's hands and scattered on the floor.

"What do you mean by this?" Mr. Bron demanded.

Thomas stumbled in his haste to pick up the teacher's things. "I didn't know you were close to the door. I'm powerful sorry, sir. I mean, my lunch pail, I forgot it, and was just hoping to get it while you were still here."

"Next time you forget something you had better mind your manners, young man." Mr. Bron glared at Thomas.

"Yes, sir, sorry, sir," Thomas said meekly. He reached for some of the papers and a couple of brown envelopes that had fallen at his feet to scoop them up. As Thomas touched one of the envelopes he felt the unmistakable outlines of coins. Written in the corner were the letters *C. M.* The charity money!

Mr. Bron had stooped over to pick up some of the books and the rest of the papers. He did not see Thomas staring at the envelope. Hastily Thomas wadded papers and envelopes together and held them out as the schoolmaster straightened up.

Mr. Bron glared at Thomas as he thrust the pile back inside the brown wrapper. "Well, what are you waiting for, sir? Get your pail and take your wretched self out at once, do you hear?"

Shaken and glad for his narrow escape, Thomas went eagerly for his lunch bucket, grabbed it, and fled. He did not see Mr. Bron glance at the corner of the envelope marked *C. M.* For a second the schoolmaster looked surprised. "So the charity money was not stolen after all! Ah, well, that shall remain my little secret." He laughed and tucked the envelope more deeply into the wrapper.

Lucas stood waiting where Thomas had left him. "What took you so long?" he asked as Thomas slowed to a walk.

"Oh, nothing much," Thomas replied. "Old Bron was still there, and I held the door for him since we was both leaving at the same time." He said nothing of the envelope to Lucas. But as they walked he whistled as if thinking to himself. It was a way Thomas had when he wasn't about to share something he knew, at least not yet.

By the time Ben reached home he wanted one thing: never to go back to school again. His father read Mr. Bron's note, then listened to Ben's explanation. His forehead creased as he heard out Ben in silence. "And that's it, Pa. When Jamie said he stole the money it was the first I heard of it. All I know is it took him long enough to admit what he did." Ben lowered his eyes to the basin of warm herbal water his mother hurried to place on the table before him. Gently she bathed his arms and covered them with wet cloths. Her face was grim.

Ben soaked his hands in the cooling water. The bruises from Mr. Bron's cane were an angry purple across the backs of his hands.

Turning back to her work at the stove Ben's mother sighed deeply. "Whatever could have possessed the boy to do such a thing?" she said.

For a moment Ben's father seemed lost in thought. He shook his head and fixed his eyes on Ben. "I believe you had nothing to do with this, son. What Jamie did can only be explained by him."

Carefully Ben's father removed the cloths from Ben's arms to look at the red welts. "When a man suffers unjustly and takes it patiently, he can wear his stripes as marks of courage, son," he said softly. "And now I'll be off to see to this matter."

"See to it then, Stewart," Ben's mother said. Her small hands gripped the kettle so hard her knuckles showed white. "Such a man deserves what's coming to him." Her face was grim. "I've half a mind to go with you myself."

"Stay here, Sarah. When Jamie comes back he'll need all the help you can give him. You'll have school in the morning, son. Better do your lessons." With that he was gone.

Ben's mother fetched a pan of corn bread and set it down with a sharp thud. "If I had my way, that man would be run out of town on a pole. Oh, dear, what am I saying?" she scolded herself, putting her hand to her mouth. The next minute her arms were about Ben and the tears she had struggled to hold back were running down her face.

"It's okay, Ma," Ben managed to say. "Leastways, now I've had one of Bron's canings, nobody can call me teacher's pet." He grinned and then winced as the back of one hand knocked against the table.

Ben finished his homework, and still Jamie had not returned. Maybe he was somewhere out there feeling sorry for himself. Good, Ben thought, flexing his stiff fingers. Serves him right. Bedtime came, but no Jamie.

Ben's mother looked worried. "I wonder if the boy has gone over to Ceil's or Luke Henry's place?" she said.

Ben scowled. "Reckon he's skulking around wishing he had never owned up."

"Why, Ben, what a thing to say!" His mother turned away from the window where she had drawn the curtains shut for the night. "What if he hadn't told the truth at all?" she asked.

"He let me take a licking first. He had no call to do that," Ben said. "And just because he's living here, Bron thinks we're in cahoots. I hope he did go back where he belongs." Ben stomped his way up to the loft and bed.

"And where would that be, Ben?" his mother asked quietly.

Ben stared at his mother. Where would Jamie go? He didn't really belong to anyone.

His father came and went out again. It was late before he returned. There was no news of Jamie. No one had seen him.

"The boy's no fool, Sarah. He'll find shelter for the night, and in the morning we'll find him."

For a long while Ben listened to the muffled voices of his parents but couldn't make out most of their words. Then as he drifted close to sleep, Ben heard his father say, "The man's like a cold stone, Sarah. His pride will bring him down one of these days. Still, he won't be caning the lads that way again, or anyone else as long as I'm here to see to it." In the silence that followed, Ben fell asleep.

On the following morning the first early December snow covered the ground with a thin white sheet, and by the look of the sky there would be more soon. By the time Ben reached school it was snowing again. Clumps of the wet stuff clung to his hair and clothes.

In the general stamping of feet and shaking off of melting snow Thomas Wickens whispered to Ben, "Wish we had a blizzard instead of just this. Don't reckon Bron'll be too pleased over yesterday. Where's your friend Jamie?"

"He is no friend of mine. I doubt if he shows up." Ben took his seat. Thomas grinned widely.

Mr. Bron looked anything but pleased. "Take out your slates, class."

Thomas had a puzzled look on his face. Like Ben and the rest he had expected to hear something about the missing money, though Thomas alone knew what.

During roll call Mr. Bron paused to look straight at Ben. "It seems our thief is absent, which leads me to think he is also a coward. I am inclined to believe, sir, that he had you and your father fooled, and that you knew nothing of his crime." He said no more. It was as close to admitting he had made a mistake that Bron would come. Next to Ben Thomas stirred restlessly. He could not believe his ears. Mr. Bron must have seen the envelope with the money, but why didn't he mention it?

Stranger still, by noon recess it was obvious that for the first time Mr. Bron had not brought his cane to school. His cold manner had not changed, and he maintained a strict classroom discipline, but the absence of the cane was new. For the rest of the day he made no mention of the envelope.

Luke Henry organized a search for young Jamie. The continuing snow covered any tracks he might have left. Worse still, a deep cold snap settled in to stay. The river froze, and wagon wheels were replaced with runners for winter travel. In spite of the cold the men looked for Jamie for three days but found no sign of him.

In the pit of his stomach Ben felt a pang of fear. Where was Jamie? Had something bad happened to him, or had he just run off to some other town away from Bellfield? All the times that he had stood up under old Jory's rampages and the canings at school he acted brave. The more Ben thought about it, the more he realized that having to admit to being a thief was more than Jamie's pride could take. But why had he done it? He could have kept quiet, and no one would have known. Maybe he had saved Ben from a worse beating. He pushed away the thought. Jamie would just have to pay the price for what he'd done, and that was that.

At the end of the week Mr. Bron announced his resignation to Deacon Blake, head of the school board. At first Ben couldn't believe the news. On the playground wild rumors mixed with a kind of joy broke out in little groups huddled to discuss the schoolmaster's leaving.

Deacon Blake was astonished. "Seems like Mr. Bron had a mighty sudden moving of the spirit to do the work of the Lord. But it don't appear right to me, leaving us with a pack of children this way," he stated to Ben's father.

"And what spirit was that, I wonder?" Ben's father mused.

The following morning Mr. Bron left with his cousin. By Monday Miss Lamer took up her old job as Bellfield's schoolteacher. She had returned to her homestead in Bellfield only the week before, leaving her young charges in the care of a well-to-do aunt in St. Paul.

As her pupils filed past her, Miss Lamer stood at the door smiling a welcome to them. Firmly but without harshness she removed a partially hidden slingshot from lanky Sam Banks's coat pocket. She put a restraining hand on Lucas Teachman's shoulder as he entered. "You may spit your chew out before you come in, Lucas. This is a schoolroom, not a pasture." Lucas took her meaning quickly, flushed red, and obeyed. Something about Miss Lamer said she would have little need for a thing like a cane but was quite in charge in her own way. Something else about her made you want to please her.

Like the others, Thomas Wickens wanted to please her too. "Miss Lamer, now that Mr. Bron is gone to help his cousin, I guess the money for charity we all collected will surely do some fine work for the poor slaves."

Miss Lamer's eyes widened. "Surely, Thomas, you know that the money the schoolchildren collected was taken by one of our students."

Thomas looked smug. "No, ma'am. Mr. Bron must have forgotten to mention that he found the envelope inside his papers. I picked it up and handed it to him myself when we kind of bumped into each other after school was out the very day it got lost."

"Are you certain, Thomas?" Miss Lamer asked.

"Sure as my name's Thomas Wickens."

"Well, then, Thomas Wickens, you and I must have a little talk after school today."

In his seat Ben sat frozen, scarcely believing what he heard. If Bron found the money, then Jamie didn't take it after all. Why did he run away then? The truth that had been nagging at the back of Ben's mind came to him clearly. Jamie had taken the blame to stop Ben's beating. Ben felt cold all over. Jamie tried to tell him, but he wouldn't listen. That's why Jamie ran off. An ache filled Ben's throat.

Jamie was out there somewhere in the bitter December cold. In spite of the cold, Miss Lamer insisted at recess that her students wrap up well and go outside for a ten-minute breath of fresh air. Ben could think of nothing else but what he had done to Jamie. He had to find him and bring him back, but how?

Sis, bundled in a heavy gray shawl, came running to stand by Ben. Her eyes were shining. "Jamie didn't do it, Ben, I knew he didn't."

"It's good news, Sis," Ben said wishing he was anywhere but here.

"Now I'm glad Luke Henry put the wedding off till tomorrow to give Jamie time to come back. He will come, don't you think? And now that everyone knows Jamie didn't steal the money we can all be together again."

Ben looked away. He wanted to say, "If it wasn't for me he would be here right now," but he didn't. Instead he patted her head and said, "I've got to go."

With an angry kick he sent a bit of packed snow flying out of his path and headed toward the school. It was his fault that Jamie had run away. The thought made him angry.

Ben's mother could hardly keep down her excitement over the good news about Jamie. "We will keep on praying God to protect him and bring him back. Now I declare, I still have pies to make, and clothes to get ready for tomorrow's wedding. And to think Christmas is right around the corner." She sounded worried at first, till she laughed and confessed, "But I can't think of a thing I'd rather do."

That night in the loft, Ben turned on his side away from Jamie's empty pallet. All evening he had thought about Jamie. At supper his father had prayed a long prayer especially for Jamie. Ben's face burned. Inside he knew whose fault it was that Jamie was not at home safe. With Jamie around, Bellfield seemed less like a strange place. Only he was no longer here. Ben buried his face in the covers.

13

The Wedding

For a little while Ben wondered if Jamie would show up for Miss Ceil's wedding. Several times he glanced toward the door hoping to see it open and Jamie's redhead poke through. His father had insisted Miss Ceil marry in the church for his first wedding in Bellfield. Christmas greens covered the window sills, the railings, every place the women could think of to hang them. Miss Ceil with her gold hair and blue dress looked truly like an angel. While Ben's father performed the ceremony, Sis held Miss Ceil's bouquet of green pine branches laced with holly berries and red ribbons. Luke Henry looked handsome in his Sunday suit. When the time came for the ring he fumbled for it in his waistcoat pocket, and when he finally fished it out he laughed and held it high for all to see.

Sam Banks, sitting next to Ben, grinned and poked Ben good naturedly. Afterward everyone went to the town hall for the celebration.

The women had gone all out for this wedding. Mounds of mashed potatoes, turkey, jellies, sausage pies, and breads of all kinds filled the tables against the walls. The wedding fruit cake was built three layers high and roped with icing pearls. Ben forgot everything else as he and Sam made for the sausage pies.

Long after Luke and Miss Ceil, showered with good wishes, left in a wagon sleigh piled with presents, the guests lingered to laugh and talk in little groups. In one of the groups Deacon Blake said loudly. "A charming bride, yes indeed. I expect Luke Henry could have made a good worker out of the orphan boy too."

Ben felt his ears burning. The man was talking about Jamie. Ben's father came up just then and said firmly, "The boy could have gone on to a fine education. He had a good mind, and as we all know now, a fine brave spirit."

That ought to give the deacon something to think about, Ben thought. Still, he cringed inside, knowing that he alone was responsible for whatever happened to Jamie. He knew what he had to do.

"Well, sir," Deacon Blake remarked, "the Good Book says do good to them as is less fortunate, and Lord knows I try. But it's my opinion, Reverend, that an orphan boy needs a strong arm to direct him, especially a redheaded one. It's the same with the Indians. It doesn't matter how much schooling you try and pour into their heads. You can't depend on them. What they understand best is a strong arm keeping them in their place." Ben didn't hear his father's answer. In a small town like Bellfield a man like Deacon Blake had a lot of power, but he had no call to talk that way about Jamie.

The men's conversation switched to the railroad, and from behind him Ben heard the deacon say, "Mark my words, when the railroad comes through, Bellfield will be the place to be. A man will be proud to call this town his home."

Disgusted, Ben yanked open the door. He would never call Bellfield home so long as men like the deacon did, not if he lived here a hundred years. A cold wetness splattered against Ben's face. The snow was falling steadily. It didn't matter. He had to find Jamie. It was only a chance, but there was one place Jamie might have gone, a place no one had thought to look. He would start there. First he would have to borrow a horse, and before that he needed to leave a note. He ran back to the church. No one had locked the door yet. Inside the small room where his father kept things he needed, Ben found paper and pen. The few folks getting into their wagons in front of the meeting hall took no notice as Ben placed the note in the wagon where his father would be sure to see it. Quickly Ben left.

He would borrow one of Luke Henry's horses. He wanted it only long enough to find Jamie. Luke Henry and Miss Ceil would understand. At least Luke Henry had two fine horses he could use beside the one Ben wanted.

When he reached Luke Henry's barn there was no sign of anyone around. Quietly Ben opened the barn door. Ben found the workhorse in its stall. Lazily it looked at Ben. Gently Ben rubbed its ears. "I need you to help find Jamie. You won't like going out in the cold, but it's something I have to do." There was no time to properly saddle the horse. They had to leave now before his folks missed him. He threw a blanket over the horse. It would have to do.

Out in the dark, snow continued to slap against his face. Ben lowered his head close to the horse's neck. "We have to stick to the river road away from town. We ought to be there in a couple of hours." He patted the horse and prodded him with his boots. "On we go, fellow. I'm sure I can find the path once we get past the fourth bend in the river. Till then we follow the river."

The horse obeyed Ben, moving slowly at first then faster as it felt the stinging wind. Ben held on with all his might. After a while he knew they were well outside of town.

The darkness seemed blacker than it had before, the wind colder, and the snow thicker. He had long since lost sight of the river. How much farther could he go in this storm? How was he supposed to see in this dark? He ought to have brought a lantern. Maybe he should have waited till morning and left before anyone was up. He pulled his hat close about his ears. He was cold, and his face stung as he lifted his head to peer into the darkness. If only he could see something familiar! The horse plodded ahead, so they must still be on the road, but if he didn't find that ghost town soon they would have to go back to Bellfield. For all he knew, maybe they were already turned around.

14

Rescue

On the afternoon Jamie left Bellfield snow fell, the first of the heavy snowstorms and bitter cold to follow. Jamie's only thought was to keep going and keep a sharp eye out for some kind of shelter before night came. A cave was his best hope. When he spotted the first dark opening of one his heart beat loudly. A bear or some other wild animal could be living in it. He waited, but nothing appeared. Moving slowly with a whispered prayer for help he approached the opening. The cave was small, but it was empty. The cave felt cold, but at least it was dry and the wind no longer buffeted him. After closing the entry way with piles of brush he covered himself with dead oak leaves and fell asleep. On the second night he found a cave similar to the first. Again he waited patiently for signs of some occupant. This time, too, he found the cave deserted and lay down to sleep, too weary even to hunt for brush to cover the opening. Sometime during the night fresh snow blew across the low entry to the cave and filled in the lower half of the opening. The storm was still blowing heavily when he awakened. Jamie rubbed his face with a bit of snow from the entry then let some melt in his mouth. Not far from the cave he found dried berries. They were like bits of hard leather in his mouth. When he had taken all the berries he could find he decided to spend the rest of the day waiting out the storm in his cave.

On the fourth day he pushed on. His empty stomach hurt, but so far he had found nothing more on the dry brittle brambles and vines. By midday his body wanted to quit, and his feet moved mechanically through the endless woods in the direction of the old Indian lands. Once he might have found help there from Joseph's people, but they were all gone now. His one hope was to find some deserted Indian home on the old reservation where he could camp. At least no one would follow him there. Determinedly he trudged on.

If only he had Jory's gun he could hunt for a deer or even a rabbit, but it too had burned in the fire with Jory and the house. Bad as it was, Jory's place had been home to him. He thought of Miss Ceil. She would be fine with Luke Henry. As for himself he had no home now, bad or good. Like Sis he was an orphan, but unlike Sis he would have to make it on his own from now on.

He tried to think how far he had come. Once or twice when he lost sight of the river he thought he recognized a rock or a certain oak tree. Maybe he was moving in circles. A body could do that and end up getting lost. He stopped to scoop up a handful of snow. It stung his hands but took away his thirst. So long as there was snow on the ground he could eat handfuls of the stuff. It didn't fill his belly, but it gave him water. How long could a body keep going on water? He wondered.

Anxiously he peered through the curtain of snow to see if there was a cave or a hollow tree. The woods grew thinner here it seemed to him. Wearily he pushed on. He had to find shelter soon.

By nightfall he no longer knew where the river was. The wind blew hard against him, and the falling snow covered him thickly. Jamie stood still. His legs ached, and his stomach cramped from hunger. With his arms wrapped around his chest he stared numbly at the blackness ahead of him. Panic surged through him. "Please help me, Lord," he prayed. "I don't know which way to go." It was so dark and he was so tired that maybe he would lie down in the snow and sleep for a while. But in his head a warning sounded like a clear voice. "No, you must keep going." Mechanically he pushed on. His panic lifted, and in its place a peaceful calm settled inside him.

He must have walked for a long while, he thought, as he put one heavy foot in front of the other. Each step was an effort. Icy snow clung to him like a blanket from head to toe. His frosted eyelids were almost closed. When he forced them open he saw only the darkness around him trying to cover him up. Then without warning he thudded heavily into something hard. After a moment of shock he could feel the thing still there, a hard solid wall of some kind, like a tree trunk. He groped with his arms and hands spread wide against it to determine where it ended. It had to be a wall.

Trembling, he kept his body close to the wall feeling for its edge. He couldn't seem to think straight, but there was something familiar under his right hand. With numb fingers he traced a crack and then a stick of some kind and a stiff cold handle—a latch! With all his strength he pulled then shoved against the door. It opened, and Jamie stumbled inside.

For a long time he lay on the floor simply listening to the wind howl outside and wondering where the folks were who lived there. After a while he pulled himself to a sitting position. His eyes felt strange, as though his face was swollen all around them. But it was too dark to see anyway. He knew he was in a log cabin, which meant somewhere in it should be a wood box and a place to make a fire. With his right shoulder against the wall he crawled his way forward, feeling for the floor and walls in front of him. When he touched cold metal he knew by its shape he had found a stove. Its door hung open, and inside he felt the gritty dust of ashes. Next to it he felt the wood box. If only he could find a matchbox he could make a fire. Some folks hung the matchbox on the wall near the wood box. As he felt the wall his fingers made out a shelf then closed around a tin box.

Shaking and fearing he might lose a single match he sat down on the floor to open the box. In the bottom he felt a handful of matches. He struck one and held it above the wood box. Before he could grab for the kindling sticks lying close to the top his match went out. Carefully Jamie stuffed the precious matchbox inside his coat pocket. His fingers felt thick and clumsy as he groped for the wood. It took him a long time to place the wood inside the stove and longer still to light it.

The old stove seemed to spring to life as Jamie fed it carefully. When he was certain it would not go out he rested by its warmth. After a while he took off his outer clothing and put it to dry by the fire. He thought he must have slept, but it was still dark outside. He groaned as he got to his feet. Weary still and aching he turned to explore the rest of the house. On the shelf where the matches had been he discovered candles and lit one.

It was a simple two-room cabin. Cobwebs covered the crude wood table and the one window. Whoever lived here must have left a long time ago, maybe years, Jamie thought.

Under a piece of rotted rag rug on the bedroom floor he found a trapdoor. Below was a root cellar that had once held the family's fruits and vegetables. It was empty now except for a dusty bag half full of seed corn. Faint with hunger he took a handful and tried to chew it. The hard kernels ground against his teeth. It would take forever to soften them, but he could roast them. He carried the bag up the ladder, closed the door, and went back to the fire.

There was nothing to pop the corn in except the

tin matchbox. Carefully Jamie emptied the matches into his pocket. Some of the corn burnt, but it tasted fine. Again and again he refilled the small tin until at last his stomach no longer felt empty. His eyes wanted to close almost before he finished, and he stumbled wearily as he banked the fire for the night.

When he awoke, the fire had died out and the room was cold. He ached in every bone but he managed to light a new fire. Why had it gone out so soon? Every bit of wood he had put in so carefully was burned to ash. Could he have slept past a whole day? He must have. Huddling close to the stove he fell asleep once more.

The morning dawned clear and cold. This time Jamie rose, built up the fire, and went outside. A few feet away stood what was left of another cabin and beyond it a frame-built store with its roof fallen in. He had stumbled into the old ghost town. Somehow, after he lost sight of the river, he must have turned back and circled toward this place. At least he knew now where he was. Years before, when times were hard in Minnesota and some folks lost everything, the town died out. Only two weeks earlier he and Ben had talked about exploring the old ghost town. "Hello," he shouted into the empty air. His was the only voice. Nothing stirred when he opened the door to the deserted store. Its shelves no longer held anything. Its counters stood bare except where pieces of the fallen roof covered them. Some of the old wood he could use for firewood.

The other cabin, smaller than the first, had nothing in it. There was a loft overhead, but someone had even taken the ladder needed to reach it.

Back at the cabin he finished another meal of corn. If he ate sparingly it might last till he reached the reservation.

During the day the cabin grew colder in spite of the stove's heat. Outside, the snow crunched icily when Jamie walked on it. The cold air burned his throat. A bitter Minnesota cold snap was coming fast and might stay for days. He would have to wait it out.

Jamie was sitting close to the fire dozing when it happened: without warning something exploded all around him. Terror gripped him as he sprang up. A burning smell assaulted his nose. Pellets were shooting everywhere. The corn! He had left his precious store of seed corn too near the stove, and a spark must have caught the bag. The bag was burning.

Quickly he dragged what was left of the bag away from the stove and out into the snow. By the time he managed to smother the flames only charred and blackened kernels remained. He knew he would need every kernel burnt or not, but the pile before him would barely do for one meager meal.

The cold hung on through the night into the next day. At least he still had firewood enough to last. The corn was gone. Only two candles were left now. For some reason he wasn't afraid, only tired from the deep pain that burned his chest and gripped his whole body when he coughed.

He lay on the floor next to the stove with the piece of rug over him. A pile of wood lay close beside him. By adding a few sticks at a time he could keep the fire going. With his eyes closed he pictured Miss Ceil's gentle face. He remembered the sound of her voice reading from the big Bible, especially the times when old Jory came home blind with whiskey, and they had barricaded themselves in the upstairs room. He could hear her now repeating the Shepherd's Psalm: "The Lord is my Shepherd, I shall not fear." Jamie thought of the pain he had caused her. Tears rolled down his face. He never meant to cause her sorrow. If only he could tell her the truth. He should never have left without telling her. He was dumber than any sheep. A cough racked him, and when it was over he felt himself drifting to sleep. The words of the Shepherd's Psalm seemed to pour over him. "Shepherd leadeth his sheep . . . No fear . . ."

He didn't know how long he slept, but he must have kept the stove going anyway, he thought. He had to keep the fire lit so Miss Ceil could start breakfast. Or was it supper? He was hot now, too hot, and tired. Then his body shook with cold, and his arms felt as heavy as the wood he lifted and put into the fire. He slept, woke, and slept again.

Outside, the wind increased to a loud mournful sound. Jamie woke and struggled to sit up. He was shivering. Was it day or night? With shaking hands he found a candle and lit it from the fire. Weak and dizzy he made his way to the window. Though he could hear the slap of snow against the window he saw nothing. "Must be a storm," he mumbled. "Better put up the light for Miss Ceil." As he stuck the candle in a bit of melted wax on the window frame a sudden chill came over him. He shook with cold as he stumbled blindly back to the stove and fell close to it. Tears seeped from his closed eyes.

Out in the storm Ben knew that he was in desperate trouble. The horse no longer moved. Snow, whipped by the wind swirled about them as he slid from the horse's back. He buried his head in the horse's side. "I never should have brought you out here like this." If only he had waited and told his father the truth. "Lord, I know I don't deserve your help after what I did to Jamie," he prayed, "and I know it was wrong to take Luke Henry's horse. Only please, don't let him die because of me. I wanted to find Jamie by myself, but I can't. I don't know which way to go or what to do," he cried. As if in answer a gust of wind pushed hard against them and the horse began to move forward slowly. Ben held on to the horse's mane. Tears stuck to his eyelashes as they plodded on in the darkness.

Ben kept his head down and his hand wrapped tightly in the horse's mane. How long they had been out in the fierce wind and cold, or where they were going, he had no idea. In spite of his warm coat he shook with cold. He pressed close to the horse for some warmth. If help didn't come soon they could die out here. He thought of the words of a Bible verse his father had taught him. It was a promise of the Lord, Pa said. He whispered the words: "I will never forsake thee."

"God does not break his promises, son," Pa had said, "and he never stops loving us." The words seemed to grip Ben like a strong hand leading him on. His teeth chattered as he repeated, "What time I am afraid I will trust in Thee, O Lord." More than once the horse stumbled, and Ben feared. He could feel its body shiver, but each time it went on. After a while, it seemed to Ben, the wind had died down. He lifted his head to peer into the night. In the dark ahead a small yellow light flickered. It had to be a house with a light in the window! It might have been the smell of smoke coming from the chimney or the tiny point of light in the window that led the horse on, but it did not stop until it reached a small cabin.

There was no answer to Ben's knock. Clearing a patch on the window he looked past the candlelight. His heart leaped at what he saw. Someone with red hair lay on the floor next to the glowing stove. Jamie!

In his haste to reach Jamie, Ben rushed into the cabin forgetting the horse out in the cold. Jamie was asleep and muttering something about sheep.

"It's me—Ben!" For several minutes Ben tried to get Jamie to open his eyes and look at him. Once he did look at Ben but seemed not to know him. Jamie's face was burning hot with fever. When he coughed, his body arched with the terrible sound. "Please, Jamie, don't die," Ben pleaded.

Someone else had seen the candlelight in the cabin window. Silently he entered the room. With a start Ben looked up to see an Indian face staring down at him.

The Indian squatted beside Jamie. "Do not be afraid." He touched Jamie's face. "Little Red Fox, I have come—your brother, John Other Day." Jamie made no response.

"His name is Jamie," Ben said.

"Yes, I know. Many years ago I knew his father. How did you come here?"

As Ben explained, the Indian, whose name was John Other Day, took leaves from a pouch and mixed them with snow in the empty tin matchbox. He brought the mixture to a boil on the stove. When it had cooled he held Jamie's head and made him drink it. "How did you find us?" Ben asked.

"I was not looking for you," John Other Day answered. "I would have passed by if you had not left your horse outside." Ben started up with a worried look on his face. "Do not worry. The horses are safe in the shelter of the barn. Our Father in the sky makes many paths meet. When my grandfather died he wished to be buried on his own land. It is not permitted to travel openly in the land, and so I journey by night. I was returning to my people when I saw your horse."

Ben knew that no Indian was allowed to leave Mr. Faribault's farm for any reason, not even to hunt. An Indian caught outside the camp could be shot. He nodded.

John Other Day shared his pemmican, a mixture of berries and dried deer meat, with Ben. Ben found it chewy but good. Several times the Indian made a warm drink for Jamie. Each time, Ben hoped Jamie would wake and recognize him, but he no longer opened his eyes. Huddled by the stove Ben must have fallen asleep, because the next thing he knew light was streaming into the cabin window.

The storm was over. John Other Day brought both his horse and Ben's to the cabin doorway. Jamie was unconscious as John Other Day carried him out wrapped in his own blanket and mounted his horse. With the boy against his chest and Ben following behind, the Indian led the way back to Bellfield.

It was Luke Henry who carried a barely breathing Jamie into the back bedroom and put him to bed. Miss Ceil sat by the bedside holding Jamie's hand and praying.

Doctor Bruder came as soon as he heard the news, but there was little he could do for the boy. "The fever's taken him hard, and his lungs are bad. He's a mighty sick lad. We'd best all keep praying."

Miss Ceil wept, and Luke laid his hand on her shoulder. "The Lord's brought him home, and we've that to be thankful for."

Miss Ceil nodded. "Yes, dearest. Thank God, the poor lamb is with us where he belongs," she said.

A weary Ben let himself be led home by John Other Day.

15

The Sickness

Y ou risked your life to bring the boys home, John Other Day, and we can never thank you enough," Ben's father said after the whole story had been told. "As for you, Ben, I believe you have learned a hard lesson."

"Yes, Pa," Ben replied meekly.

Turning to John Other Day, his pa said, "I will see you to Faribault. It is far too dangerous for you to go alone."

"Yes," Ben's mother agreed. "And you must take with you some food and blankets. It is the least we can do." When they were gone Ben slept and knew nothing more for the rest of the day. The smell of fried bacon woke him. He lay still, remembering all that had happened. What if Jamie died? There had been no chance to tell Jamie that Bron took the money, or to tell him that he was sorry.

The worst winter in years gripped Minnesota, hitting the town of Bellfield hard. Bitter cold winds swept down from the north and blew across the countryside. Thomas Wickens's cat's tail froze and broke off. The mounds of earth piled all around the base of the schoolhouse against the cold were frozen solid.

Ben shivered in the drafty schoolroom in spite of his woolens. He tried to keep his mind on what Miss Lamer was saying, but worry about Jamie kept coming back.

The classroom looked almost empty. Only a handful of students had escaped coughs, croup, and for some even worse, the dreaded diphtheria. Jamie was still out sick, and Ben had not been allowed to see him yet. Even Tessie Blake was sick. Ben looked up as Miss Lamer stopped her teaching to cough. By the end of the day her voice sounded more like a throaty whisper than her own.

Darkness fell early these days, and Ben's mother had already lit the lamps by the time Ben finished his after-school chores. The sound of a rider stopping at the cabin brought them both to the door. It wouldn't be Ben's pa. He had taken the wagon sled and was not expected home till late. It was Thomas Wickens's father. Bits of ice clung to his beard and eyebrows. The rest of him was almost hidden in heavy wraps. Ben closed the door behind him as Mr. Wickens stepped into the room. "Evening, ma'am," he said removing his ice-laden hat. "Peers like Miss Lamer's down sick for a spell. I'm here to pass the word won't be no school tomorrow. She is figuring to be back on Monday. Leastwise, it ain't diphtheria like the Klem family is all down with." He glanced at the kitchen table set for two and added, "Reckon the preacher's over to the Blakes. His missus and the girl's mighty sick, I hear."

Ben's mother motioned Mr. Wickens to a chair. "Please, sit down, and let me get you a cup of hot coffee."

"Can't be staying, but I'd sure be glad for the coffee, thank you kindly. Got to make some more calls."

"Yes, of course, and you probably want to be on your way before it gets any colder out there," Ben's mother said.

"Coldest winter on record," Mr. Wickens stated. "Reckon there's more than a few folks won't make it through this sickness."

With a heaviness in her voice Ben's mother agreed that the cold was the worst she had ever seen and that the sickness was widespread. Her forehead creased with worry when she shut the door behind Mr. Wickens. "Ben, you sure you're feeling okay?" she asked. She touched her hand to his face.

"Never felt better. Thomas Wickens, Will Coster, and me were the only fellows left in school." He reached for his jacket. "Think I'll take a run over and see how Jamie's doing."

"You'll do no such thing, Benjamin Stewart Able. I was there this morning with a pot of stew, and both Ceil and Sis were feeling poorly. Luke Henry has his hands full." Firmly she marched Ben to the table and handed him a bowl of shriveled apples. "You can start peeling those apples for supper. Jamie, poor lad, is doing as well as can be expected."

She looked at Ben thoughtfully for a moment. "I guess we ought to be grateful that Bellfield has a good doctor living here. Lots of places don't have one."

Supper had been over for two hours when Ben's father came in, his face gray with tiredness. All day he had visited sick families. "The Landers lost young Tom to the croup today," he said.

"Oh, no, Stewart." His mother's eyes filled with tears, and Ben felt a lump in his throat for the small lad who had toddled about merrily only weeks before.

While his father sat by the fire, his head nodding over the open Bible on his lap, Ben quietly climbed to the loft to check on his arrow collection. Cold seeped through the cracks in the loft walls, and Ben was about to go down when someone knocked at the door.

It was Deacon Blake, half-covered with ice. "Hope you don't mind my coming around this time of night, but there's something I'm needing to tell you, Pastor."

Startled, Ben's mother put her hands to her mouth. "Oh, dear, Tess has not taken a turn for the worse? Surely not your dear wife?"

"No, no," the deacon said quickly. "The missus is coming around. Doc says she'll be all right. Tess, well, she's hanging in there. The Lord knows she's a fighter." His voice grew husky and he cleared his throat. "I can't stay long, but there is something I knew I had to do, and do quickly."

Ben's father motioned Deacon Blake to a seat by the fire and helped him with his coat. His mother hurried to place a hot cup of coffee in the man's hands. "You'll be needing this to warm up a bit," she said. "I'm sure you two will excuse me. There's a bit of quilt to mend in the bedroom." With the small foot-warming stove full of hot coals she left the two men to themselves.

As the door closed behind her, Ben heard his father gently ask, "How can I help? It's Tessie, isn't it?"

A sudden warmth filled Ben's face. He was trapped in the loft where he couldn't help overhear the conversation below.

Deacon Blake shook his head and covered his eyes with his hands. Ben's father sat down near the man. "Let me go back to your house with you, man," he pleaded.

"There is nothing anyone can do. I wouldn't have come now, but after you left this afternoon, I kept thinking." He paused then went on. "I've come to make things right with God." His voice broke as the words poured out. "If God takes my little girl, it'll serve me right. All that talk about Indians I've done? Well, it's all rot. I've been in on a scheme to buy up all the reservation land we could lay our hands on. Buy cheap, and nobody the wiser. Three years ago I knew the Indians were being cheated out of food and money meant for them, but I kept still. What the Indians did was wrong, but maybe it could have all been prevented. Only, I did nothing." He buried his head in his heads; his voice choked with sobs.

In the loft Ben crept silently to his bed. He didn't want to hear any more. Maybe Jamie's folks would not have died if the Indians had gotten the food and things they had been promised. The deacon should have told the government what was happening to the Indians. Now would Tess die too?

Then guilt struck Ben's own conscience. He had blamed Jamie for something he didn't do and never gave him a chance to explain. He pulled the covers over his head to shut out the sounds from below, but he knew from his father's voice that he was praying for the deacon. Ben didn't hear the deacon leave.

A week went by, and still there was no letup in the sickness that touched both town and countryside. Tessie Blake had made it through the crisis time, but Will Coster did not, and Ben mourned his death. Family after family was touched with sickness. Ben helped his mother prepare large pots of soup for families where there was no one well enough to tend to the cooking. From morning till late at night his father visited the sick and bereaved.

The day finally came when there was only one new case. A change in the weather brought slightly warmer temperatures. Ben finished his chores and dumped the last load of firewood into the kitchen box. Supper was over. At the stove his mother stirred the stew she was keeping hot for his father, who was always late these days. Ben heard the wagon pull up to the cabin. His mother set out a bowl of hot stew. But no one came, and the stew began to cool. "Run out and help your pa before this stew is cold," his mother ordered.

His father was leaning against the horse. "Let me help, Pa," he called. There was no response.

By the time Ben reached the wagon his father had no strength to stand by himself. It was all Ben could do to help support his heavy weight into the house. "Ma, open the door! It's Pa! He's sick."

His mother ran from the cabin to help. Between the two of them they managed to get his tall frame inside and onto the bed. "Quick, Ben, fetch Doc Bruder. Hurry!" she cried.

Ben turned the bewildered horse back toward town and lowered his chin into his muffler against the night wind. As he rounded the road into town, the yellow light shining from the front windows of the doctor's house eased his fear. The doctor was home.

"Doctor Bruder, it's me, Ben Able," he cried as he pounded the door. In a moment the door was flung wide.

"Come in, boy. Don't stand there letting the wind in." The doctor, a middle-aged man with a graying beard, stood aside for Ben to enter. He listened gravely as Ben pleaded for him to come.

"Collapsed, did he? Not surprised, the way that man's been going night and day tending to folks. Seems like everywhere I went your father was no more than a step behind me, and sometimes there before me." Gruff as the doctor's manner was unless you were sick, folks respected him.

Ben knew his father liked the doctor. During these long weeks of sick calls, he had told them tales of the doctor's tireless care. The doctor was ready to leave, and Ben took his bag. "I'll drive you, sir, and bring you back, too, when you're ready. It'll save you some."

With a look of surprise, the doctor eyed Ben. "Well, can't say I wouldn't like to have a driver, son. But my old Jessie wouldn't like it a bit. Seems like that horse knows when I set foot out of this house. Got her trained so she'll bring the buggy back home and me sound asleep in it every time." With that he hurried them both out into the night.

The room felt hot to Ben as he followed his mother and the doctor into the cabin bedroom. "Keep the stove going, Ben," his mother called over her shoulder. Ben hesitated. He wanted to go to his father's bedside, but a glance at the shivering, shaking form in the bed made him hurry to the kitchen.

Carefully he poked at the already blazing fire, added a few sticks, and watched them catch. The box of firewood seemed low to him. They would need lots more. He snatched up a lantern, lit it, and went to fetch more wood. An indignant snorting greeted him. The horses! He had forgotten the horses.

The poor animals were cold and tired. "Come on, Jessie," he urged the annoyed mare, "you can just bed down in the barn too until Doc comes for you."

By the time Ben entered the kitchen with his fresh load of wood, the doctor was standing talking to his mother. As Ben came in, he paused.

With a grave look the doctor said, "I expect this will be a long night for all of us. Your pa is a mighty sick man. Suppose you could bed down old Jessie out in your barn, son?"

"Already did, sir," Ben answered. "What's the matter with Pa?"

"Well, for one thing, he's plum worn out. On top of that it seems he's got the worst case of measles I've ever seen in a grown man." The doctor chuckled.

"Measles!" Ben couldn't believe it.

"Likely he was exposed over at the Sloanes," the doctor stated. "All five of their youngsters are down with it. Lucky for you, your ma tells me, you've already had 'em." He sat down at the table, and Ben's mother went to the stove to fetch the coffee pot. Gratefully the doctor took the steaming cup she offered him. "Thank you, Sarah."

His mother sat down at the table and poured herself a cup. "Come and sit, son," she said, patting the chair beside her. Ben hung up his coat and sat down.

"You see," the doctor went on to explain, "it's a combination of exhaustion and high fever that's the problem here. I expect before morning we'll know one way or the other."

Ben felt his stomach sink. "Is Pa going to die?"

"Not if I have anything to say about it and the good Lord is willing," the doctor said gruffly. He drained his coffee cup and placed it on the table. "Now I'm off to my patient. You try and get some sleep. If I need you I'll call."

Ben's mother shook her head. "I couldn't sleep. Let me watch him, and you can show me what to do while you lie down for a little. I promise I'll wake you the minute there's a change."

The doctor nodded. "A blanket by the fire will do me fine. He won't wake up for an hour anyway. After that we'll see."

"Ben, you fetch an extra quilt from the loft for the doctor and fix up the sofa, dear. I'll not have you sleeping on the floor," she insisted, turning to the doctor.

Within minutes the doctor was indeed asleep, his snoring a sure sign. Ben tiptoed past to his father's bedside. His mother, seated close to the bed, reached out her arm to him. With the other she replaced the cool cloth his father's fevered tossing had knocked off.

"We need to pray and trust our heavenly Father's love," she whispered.

Ben nodded, but his thoughts whirled. They should never have come out here in the first place.

As if reading his mind, his mother said softly, "We're a long way from New York now, dear. Your father and I know it hasn't been easy, and we're all trying hard. When the call came for your father to come here, we were sure it was God's will. And whatever happens, nothing's going to change that.

Your father and I love you dearly." She held him close.

"Are you afraid?" Ben whispered.

"Yes, oh yes, son. I'm so afraid." Tears ran down her face. "Like you were when you tried to find Jamie in that storm. It's what we do with our fears that counts," she whispered. "How often have we heard your father say, 'When I am afraid, I will put my trust in Thee, O Lord.' And that's what I'm doing, dear, what we both need to do."

His father groaned, and his mother quickly turned to him. Ben watched her change the cloth and smooth the damp hair from his forehead. "Please, God, make him better. Please, don't leave us alone here." A sudden sound in his father's breathing, a raspy labored sound, startled them both. Clearly something had gone wrong.

"Wake the doctor, Ben, wake him," his mother commanded.

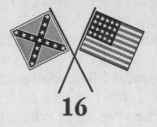

16

A Change in the Deacon

The doctor worked quickly to construct a small tent made with a sheet over the head of the bed where Ben's father lay breathing noisily. Ben's mother filled an iron kettle with steaming water and placed it at the bedside. All night the doctor sat by his patient. Under the tent warm, moist air collected. "We've got to keep that steam going," the doctor ordered, "so he can breathe easier." At the stove Ben brought fresh pots of water to the boil ready for his mother to refill the kettle.

Sometime during the night he leaned his head on his arms at the table. When he opened his eyes he was on the sofa. Daylight shone in the window above him. His mother and the doctor were seated at the kitchen table eating breakfast. He sat up slightly dazed.

"About time you woke up, son," the doctor teased. "Thought maybe your ma's bacon might just do the trick." He winked and went back to eating with gusto.

"Pa?" Ben asked, looking at his mother.

"He's asleep, breathing good, and the fever's broken," she said.

The doctor stopped eating to add, "That means, son, it looks like the Lord plans to keep your pa right here a spell longer. Of course, he's weak as a baby right now, and I don't reckon he'll be preaching or running around the countryside for some time yet."

"It's the best Christmas present we could have," his mother said.

"Well so it will be," the doctor said. He held his coffee cup out as Ben's mother poured. "Thank you kindly. I guess Christmas is going to be kind of quiet around here this year. Now what your man needs is plenty of rest, quiet, and a light diet till he's feeling stronger. The measles will run its course; it's pneumonia we don't want settling in. He's to stay put; no work of any kind till I say so."

"Right," Ben's mother said firmly.

Ben grinned. Keeping his tall, restless father down, measles or not, might be harder than the doctor knew.

Word that the preacher was sick spread quickly. A steady stream of well-wishers brought gifts of freshly made breads, nourishing soups, custards, jams, even some homemade remedies guaranteed to help the invalid's recovery.

"I declare, we'll never eat up all this food," Ben's mother said. Mrs. Wickens had just stepped in to leave a bowl of custard for the pastor. "Still, it is lovely to feel so accepted by folks," she said and smiled at Ben.

School started again with a handful of students

whose number steadily grew as the week went on. These days Ben rolled out of bed early to do the chores before breakfast. He had just left the cabin when the sound of an axe rang clear in the cold sharp air. He hurried past the barn and stopped short at the sight of Deacon Blake chopping away at the woodpile.

"Morning, Ben. Thought your ma might need an extra hand with some of this while your pa's down. Reckon you have all you can do with chores now that school's on again."

Ben's face colored as he remembered what he had overheard the night the deacon came to see his pa. "Much obliged to you, sir," he said. "We been lighting into the woodpile pretty heavy these days keeping the place warm while pa's sick."

"Well, don't you worry none. There'll be plenty enough." The deacon lifted his axe to chop at the log in front of him.

"Guess I'll be going on to the barn, then," Ben said. He almost forgot to ask about Tessie. "I hope Mrs. Blake and Tessie are better," he added.

"Thank the Lord, that they surely are," the deacon said. He continued chopping and began to whistle. Ben frowned. Deacon Blake could have hired someone to chop wood for him any time he needed it, and here he was doing the work himself for his pa. And whistling too. It just wasn't like Deacon Blake.

Ben arrived at school early. Sis hurried toward him, her lunch pail swinging wildly at her side.

"Morning, Sis. Any news?"

Sis shook her head. "Doctor Bruder says the pneumonia has left him very weak. No one can go near him 'cept Miss Ceil and Luke." Her small mouth trembled.

Ben patted her arm. "He'll be okay soon, you'll see. Doc Bruder is a good man." He walked her into school and reached her lunch pail up onto the shelf for her.

Tessie Blake was back, a little peaked looking and, as usual, surrounded by admirers. A few of the younger children were absent, and one or two older ones. Two empty seats drew Ben's eyes—Will Coster's and Jamie's. A lump filled Ben's throat as he thought of Will's funeral. Ben had seen the tears on old Grandpa Coster's face. Will was his favorite grandson.

Miss Lamer, her voice clear and strong once more, called for attention. " I have an announcement, class," she said. "Most of you know that each year the town offers a prize for the best essay. The contest this year is on the subject of honor. Now, I'd like you upper forms to be thinking about this. I shall expect some fine papers."

"Honor," whispered Thomas Wickens to Ben. "Guess that won't be hard. Didn't good old General Sherman hand over Savannah as a Christmas present to the Union? Plenty about honor there." Ben didn't answer. Most likely everybody would write about the war and the brave troops, himself included. He glanced at Tessie Blake who was writing on her slate. She was probably making plans already.

The worst of the cold was over, and the sun seemed stronger after school than it had only a week before. Ben and Sam Banks walked steadily toward town. "You sure Mr. Dolan wants two boys to help him?" Ben questioned.

"Yup, two, he said. Asked if I knew anybody, and I told him you'd be glad to help. Course," Sam continued, "it's only till he can get somebody to take Miss Ceil's place. I can sure use the money."

"Me too," Ben agreed.

Mr. Dolan seemed in a big hurry to put them both to work. "Haven't had a minute's time to set this place to rights ever since the sickness set in. Everybody needs supplies. The women are starting to sew up for the spring, and there's stock to be put out and sorted." Hastily he showed the boys where to dust and how to count stock.

Ben had never been behind the counters of a store like this one. Its shelves held everything from bolts of material and buttons to leather shoes. Nails and tools and barrels of things stood near brooms and hoes. Whole bins of candy, flour, coffee, rice, and other foodstuffs took up half the storeroom. In the very back a small room served as Mr. Dolan's office. Stacked to the ceiling were dozens of household items including pots and pans. Gingerly Ben picked up a china cup, dusted the space around it, and set it back. He concentrated so hard he didn't hear anyone come in.

"Afternoon, George. See you've got yourself two new helpers." Deacon Blake again.

Mr. Dolan hurried past Ben and Sam to the counter. The deacon was a wealthy man and spent generously. "And what can I do for you today, Mr. Blake?" Mr. Brown asked eagerly.

"You can give me ten sacks of flour, ten of corn-meal, ten cones of sugar, and twenty red wool blankets. You got any of that deer meat sausage? I'll take whatever you've got left, and throw in a dozen sacks of hard candy while you're at it." He paused to look at his list.

Mr. Brown stood listening, with his eyebrows raised and his mouth open. "You planning on a big trip or something?" he asked.

Deacon Blake laughed. "No, sir. These supplies are for the Indians up on Faribault's land. Seems they've had a harder winter than most folks."

"Well, ain't that nice of you, Deacon. Peers to me like Mr. Faribault has got himself a pack of trouble. Ought to send them all up to Nebraska and let the government take care of them." He continued writing down the order in the big account book as he spoke. "Guess they would settle down with their own kind one way or the other."

In a slow and deliberate voice Deacon Blake said, "Those Indians haven't done us any wrong. Have you forgotten, man, that some of them risked their lives to help white settlers? They're a peaceful people who just happen to be paying for the wrongs of a few Indians and of some of us whites. I'm done with land grabbing and cheating, as God is my witness, and I don't aim to stand by and let them suffer if I can help any."

Mr. Dolan laid a sack of cornmeal on the counter. He didn't look at Deacon Blake. "Peers like you've had a change of mind," he said.

The deacon laughed, then said in a softer tone, "Call it a change of heart, George. Look, I'll be back for this later. I've got some other business to tend to in town."

Sam and Ben had both stopped working while the deacon and Mr. Dolan talked. The look on Sam's face was pure astonishment.

As he passed the boys the deacon stopped and looked hard at Sam. "Don't ever pay to count out the Lord, son. The good Lord can do some powerful work on a body. Don't you forget that. And by the way, if you two boys are interested, I just may have a summer job for you. We'll be needing good lads like you as water boys and fetchers when the railroad work starts. You let me know, boys."

When the door closed behind him, Ben let out a small whoop. "The railroad! Did you hear that, Sam?"

"I heard it, and I can't believe that was the deacon," Sam replied.

Mr. Dolan shook his head. "Can't figure what's got into the man, but something sure as fire has. All this for a bunch of Indians." He pitched another sack onto the growing pile. "It's his money, and if that's the way he wants to spend it, that's fine with me." He turned to Ben. "Boy, back of that stack of blankets you'll find a box of old stock; see if there's any red ones left in there. No need of wasting new ones on Indians."

Ben gritted his teeth and went to find the blankets.

17

An End and a Beginning

The class was all ears as Miss Lamer held up the winning essay. "Class, I am pleased to announce our winner for the essay contest on honor is Miss Tessie Blake." Tessie beamed.

Thomas Wickens poked Ben in the ribs and whispered, "Bet her ma helped her." Ben raised his eyebrows in a gesture of disgust. He knew Tessie Blake could write her own essay and do a good job. On Thursday night at the school program, Tessie read her essay. Before she began she paused and looked at the audience. "This year I learned the meaning of real honor from my father," she said. Ben sat, up all attention. What did Tessie mean?

"My father," she read "will always be the one who first showed me an example of real honor." What followed was an honest account of the wrongs Ben had heard the night Deacon Blake came to talk to his father. The roomful of town folks was as still as stone. "To sum up," Tessie read, "my father made mistakes and he admitted them, then he did what he could to help the Indians still left around here. He did the honorable thing, even when it meant he would have to face his former partners and their scorn. He was not ashamed to admit his wrong openly and shoulder the blame." A slow trickle of tears slid down Tessie's face. For a moment she stopped reading, then took a deep breath and went on. "Some folks cover up their sins, but the man who confesses them and does what he can to right them knows the real meaning of honor. Thank you, Pa," she whispered, "for teaching me. I love you, Pa."

Mr. Blake stood to his feet. A sob choked his voice as he reached his daughter and clasped her in his arms. The audience had risen, too, and was clapping loudly.

As the deacon and Tessie came down the aisle, Ben's father reached out to hug them both. "Welcome home, brother," he said.

Ben swallowed hard. His throat felt dry, and his eyes burned. Everything Tessie said about honor pointed a finger at him. Nobody else knew that the day of his beating he had refused to let Jamie explain. He had blamed him and told him to go away. He was the reason Jamie ran away. What if Jamie took a turn for the worse and died? He had to see him. But what if Jamie didn't want to see him?

He looked across at Sis, who waved a small hand at him. Her trusting eyes made him squirm. He was supposed to be Jamie's best friend. With drooping shoulders Ben hurried out into the night. Tomorrow he would talk to Sis.

At school recess Sis came to stand by Ben. Her

small face looked at him trustingly. Ben hunched his shoulders and lowered his face as though deep in thought. He had to tell Jamie he was sorry. He never really meant for him to run away. Ben swallowed hard. He was no different from Thomas Wickens, who had let Jamie be called a thief when he knew all the time Bron had the money.

Ben stared at Sis. "Sis, there's something I have to do." He put his hand on the girl's shoulder and led her away to a quiet part of the yard. "Tonight, Sis, I'm coming to see Jamie."

Sis looked at Ben somberly. "I know, Ben, you and Jamie are best friends." Her words stung Ben. "But why do you want to come tonight? Maybe by next week, the doctor says, he can have visitors."

Ben wet his lips. "Sis, I've got to see Jamie. There's something he needs to know. I can't tell you, and you'll just have to trust me." Ben looked down at his feet and then back at Sis. "But this can't wait. I've got to see him, and you can help." Sis hesitated, then nodded. Her face was all trust now. "First, tell me where Jamie's room is."

Sis thought for a moment. "Jamie's room gets the sun in the morning first thing, but to get to it you have to pass Luke and Miss Ceil's room."

Ben nodded. "There's got to be a way. What about Jamie's window?"

Her eyes grew bright. "Dr. Bruder says the fresh air is good for Jamie, so it's open most warm days now, but I think it's shut at night. There is an old tree close to the house with a couple of branches that reach near the window," she added. "Reckon the big one might hold you."

"Good girl," Ben said. "That's it, then. I'll wait till everyone 's asleep. You just make sure the window's open, Sis. Can you do that?"

Her years as an orphan had taught Sis a good deal of independence. She smiled confidently at Ben. "I tiptoed in twice to see Jamie when nobody was around. Guess I can leave the window open enough so's you could lift it."

"Thanks," Ben said. The recess bell rang, and Sis hurried off, her braids flopping wildly. Ben followed slowly. He hoped his plan would work.

Ben hadn't counted on company. "I promised Mrs. Blake that as soon as she was well enough we'd celebrate together. You and Tessie will have lots to talk about," his mother said as she stirred a pot of beans on the stove. "Would you please run down to the root cellar and fetch the rest of those dried apples, Ben?" she asked. Ben swallowed hard. What would he say to Tessie Blake?

At supper his mother brought up the subject of Tessie's winning essay and complimented her on it. Ben couldn't help agreeing with her, and he meant it. Tessie smiled at him, and Ben felt his face grow hot. Maybe he had said too much. After supper his father suggested Ben show Tessie his arrowhead collection. Ben groaned inwardly as he climbed the ladder to the loft. What did a girl like Tessie care about an old arrowhead collection?

Tessie's black eyes flashed with interest as Ben

opened the tin box that held the arrowheads. She picked up one with curious scratchings along its base. "May I?" she asked. Ben nodded. "What a beauty!" Tessie exclaimed. "I saw one like that when my pa took me to visit the reservation. I ought to show you my collection sometime."

Ben stared at her. He had no idea Tessie collected arrowheads. "You mean you like arrowheads?" he stammered. It was a dumb question, and he knew it.

From the kitchen table where the folks still lingered over coffee, Deacon Blake said, "Didn't Tessie tell you she's been collecting Indian artifacts since she was knee high to a grasshopper?" The deacon laughed and went back to his conversation with Ben's father.

Ben blushed and reached for the box now on Tessie's lap. "Guess these aren't much to look at," he said.

Tessie lifted her eyes to Ben. Her face was thinner and still a little paler than before her illness. It made her dark eyes even bigger. To Ben she looked like one of the pale princesses in an old illustrated book of tales he once read.

"You are wrong, Ben," she said firmly. "At least three of these are excellent specimens. It's true I do have a lot, some like the rest of these, but these three are especially fine." Ben gulped. For the next several minutes they talked about Indian arrowheads. By the time the Blakes left, Ben had almost forgotten about Jamie.

It was late, and he still had to get out of the house.

Ben was almost to the top of the ladder, his thoughts in a whirl, when his father called him.

"Son, I was over to Luke Henry's place this afternoon. Jamie is doing so well that Doc Bruder says he can have a little company tomorrow, and he is asking for you."

Ben swallowed hard. His face burned as he thought of the plan he almost carried out. "Thanks, Pa. Guess I sure will make a visit." Luke Henry had understood about the horse and forgiven Ben, though Ben had to promise never to do such a thing again. Now he would ask Jamie's forgiveness. In his heart he promised himself to go first thing in the morning. He could only hope someone would shut Jamie's window. As he clambered onto the loft a thought struck him. He had been so determined to see Jamie, it had not occurred to him that Jamie might ask to see him. But why? He couldn't think of a reason.

He was still puzzled when Miss Ceil, pert and pretty in a blue wool dress, led him into Jamie's room and left the two of them alone. Jamie's flaming red hair was the same, but the rest of him was a thin shadow of the Jamie Ben remembered.

"Hi," Jamie said. "Been a long time. Guess you know about Bron taking the charity money." Ben nodded. "I sure played the fool on that one, lighting out without a word to Luke or anyone."

Ben's face grew hot. "I'm the fool one. I should have known enough to listen to you explain in the first place. I reckon you nearly lost your life on account of me, and I'm sorry."

Jamie grinned up at Ben. "So, we both messed up. That beating you took from Bron was enough to muddle anyone's thinking. I ought to know." He extended a thin hand to Ben. "I'm right glad I'm here, thanks to you. Want to shake on it?" Ben grasped Jamie's hand and shook it firmly.

"How did you figure on finding me in that old ghost town?" Jamie asked. For several minutes Ben described all the events of that night. When he finished, Jamie told his part of the story.

"If you had gone by the town on to the old reservation," Ben said, "I never would have found you."

"Reckon so," Jamie replied. "And if Luke Henry's horse didn't lead you to the cabin you would have missed me anyway." Ben was silent for a moment as he remembered John Other Day's words: "Our Father in the sky makes many paths to cross."

"Guess for a city fellow you did mighty fine," Jamie said then grinned at Ben. "Soon as I'm up," he went on, "I'll show you an even bigger ghost town across the river north of Bellfield. We ought to cross the river while the ice is still thick."

Ben smiled. Propped against the pillows Jamie looked thin and pale and here he was making plans like he wasn't sick at all. "Maybe Bron was right about one thing," Ben said. Jamie looked at him with narrowed eyes. "Your sure do get your spunk from somewhere. Guess it must be that red

hair of yours." He laughed, and Jamie smiled broadly. The hour went by quickly as the boys made
plans.

It was time to go, and Jamie waved a thin hand
to Ben. "Won't nothing keep me down now, Ben."

When Ben left he felt lighter than he had for
weeks. Jamie would get well; he knew it! Suddenly
he remembered New Year's Day had come and
gone, and this was 1865. Folks were saying this year
should see the end of the war with the South. That
meant Sam Banks's older brother would be coming home from the army, and a lot of other Bellfield men too. It would be a good year. He could
feel it! He pulled his hat close to shut out the cold.
Pa said Minnesota winters had a way of hanging
on. Maybe so, but spring always followed sooner
or later.

On his way past the snowcovered cornfield he
saw the grave marker for Zack. Its top stuck out
above the snow, and he stopped to clear a space
around it. He thought of Zack buried somewhere
in the Blue Ridge Mountains. Nobody really knew
where. Sometimes he wondered if maybe Zack
wasn't dead but lost in the mountains.

Whether he was dead or alive, Ben would not forget him. "But, Lord," he whispered, "a body's just
got to have a friend, and I guess there is Jamie now.
I reckon Zack would understand." He could almost
hear Zack saying, "That redheaded orphan's got real
grit."

The wind blew a strong gust, and Ben straight-

ened the wooden cross. The marker wasn't much,
but it was Zack's. Ben brushed the snow from the
words *Gone Home*, then made his way toward the
small cabin where the empty window boxes
waited for spring to make them bloom.